Sara's eyes widened before shutting tight.... Oh, my God, I just made an indecent proposal! I can take anything but laughter—please, please don't let him laugh in my face.

Several seconds passed and Sean didn't laugh. The only sound she could hear was the audible rasp of his labored breathing.

"Is this seduction inspired by compassion, Sara?" Sean drawled.

Her eyes shot open at his husky question. "No! Oh, definitely not. This is lust, mad, bad, insatiable lust!"

KIM LAWRENCE lives on a farm in rural Wales. She runs two miles daily and finds this an excellent opportunity to unwind and seek inspiration for her writing! It also helps her keep up with her husband, two active sons and the various stray animals that have adopted them. Always a fanatical consumer of fiction, she is now equally enthusiastic about writing. She loves a happy ending!

Kim Lawrence

THE GROOM'S ULTIMATUM

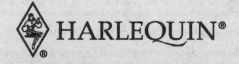

HARLEQUIN®

TORONTO • NEW YORK • LONDON
AMSTERDAM • PARIS • SYDNEY • HAMBURG
STOCKHOLM • ATHENS • TOKYO • MILAN • MADRID
PRAGUE • WARSAW • BUDAPEST • AUCKLAND

ISBN 0-373-18832-3

THE GROOM'S ULTIMATUM

First North American Publication 2004.

Copyright © 2002 by Kim Lawrence.

All rights reserved. Except for use in any review, the reproduction or
utilization of this work in whole or in part in any form by any electronic,
mechanical or other means, now known or hereafter invented, including
xerography, photocopying and recording, or in any information storage
or retrieval system, is forbidden without the written permission of the
publisher, Harlequin Enterprises Limited, 225 Duncan Mill Road,
Don Mills, Ontario, Canada M3B 3K9.

All characters in this book have no existence outside the imagination of
the author and have no relation whatsoever to anyone bearing the same
name or names. They are not even distantly inspired by any individual
known or unknown to the author, and all incidents are pure invention.

This edition published by arrangement with Harlequin Books S.A.

® and TM are trademarks of the publisher. Trademarks indicated with
® are registered in the United States Patent and Trademark Office, the
Canadian Trade Marks Office and in other countries.

www.eHarlequin.com

Printed in U.S.A.

CHAPTER ONE

'Is SHE asleep?'

Sean slowed, and stopped, recognising the voice of his mother's second husband, George Stean.

'*George…?*' Almost too late to avoid impact with a heavy oak beam, he ducked as he pushed the iron latch on the half-open heavy oak door open and stepped through.

Some people would no doubt envy the family who were fortunate enough to occupy the historically significant Spring Hurst Hall, which came complete with a colourful documented history, acres of original panelling, miles of echoey corridors and a resident ghost—but Sean wasn't one of them. He found the oak panelling dark and oppressive, the rooms too small, the ceilings too low and, besides, he preferred a house where a moment's lapse in concentration didn't leave anyone over six feet with a bad case of concussion!

Sean Garvey, a lean and athletic six feet five, was several inches into that danger zone.

If he put his personal preferences to one side it wasn't hard to see why the place was considered one of the most historically important Tudor houses still in private ownership in this part of the country—private, but not always a home. It had been through several reincarnations, most recently as a girls' boarding-school when George had bought it and set about returning it to its original glory. This had happened about ten years ago and had coincided with his *first* retirement and his marriage to Sean's mother, Hilary.

Nobody had been particularly surprised, least of all his new wife, when George had tired of playing country squire after about six months. He was a dynamo of a man who had built up his media empire from scratch. Sean had never been able to imagine his stepfather relinquishing control to a younger man. In fact until his mother's illness had been diagnosed a few months earlier Sean had been convinced the only way anyone would get George Stean out from behind his big desk was feet first, but since that moment he had devoted himself to her to the exclusion of everything else.

Sean had never been in favour of the match, he still found George one of the most difficult people he knew, but if he'd ever doubted the older man's feelings for his second wife he no longer did. Not even the problems over the launch of the new digital channel had made him leave her side.

'She was asleep,' Sean confirmed as he entered one of the few rooms in the house that wasn't heavily panelled—the uneven walls here were colour-washed a soft pastel colour. The antique lace drape over the half-tester bed, sprigged cotton fabric at the mullioned windows and faint flowery scent in the air proclaimed this a female domain—the mix of dog-eared stuffed toys and cosmetics proclaimed the occupant as someone who still remembered her childhood.

The older man nodded and put the threadbare teddy in his hands back on the pillow. 'She had a really bad night,' he revealed tiredly as he got up from the bed.

'Which means you did too.' Despite round-the-clock nursing care, he knew George didn't sleep if Hilary was awake.

'I wish it were me!'

Sean heard the ring of sincerity in the older man's cry and his rather hard grey eyes softened. 'You and me both,' he replied grimly, recognising extremely well the impotent anger his stepfather exuded.

Anger and helplessness were feelings Sean had been struggling to contain himself since his mother had been diagnosed with leukaemia. In fact it frequently seemed to him that it was Hilary herself who had come to terms best with her diagnosis.

He found her resilience and bravery extraordinary and humbling, but he sometimes worried she was putting on an act for their benefit—where was her anger? Maybe he had enough for them both…?

'Have you told Sara yet?' he asked, ignoring once more the edict that that particular name was not to be mentioned in George's presence. It seemed a safe bet Sara was on his mind as he was in her old room.

No matter how much George ranted and raged about her unnatural behaviour—and he did!—Sean knew that George's estranged daughter was and always would be adored by the ageing media tycoon.

George shook his head, his mouth hardening. 'It's a bit difficult to tell someone something when you haven't seen them for eighteen months,' he defended belligerently.

Sean gave a disbelieving smile. 'You expect me to believe you don't know where she is…?'

If he knew George, and he did, the man probably had a report on his desk that told him what the girl—or was it woman?—had eaten for breakfast. Sara's bitter accusations that her father was a control freak had not been totally unfounded.

The older man gave a concessionary shrug. He picked up a framed photo; his daughter complete with braces, her bright hair tied up in pigtails, gazed back at him clutching a big shiny gymkhana cup.

'She was so much easier when she was that age.' He sighed nostalgically.

Sean, who doubted Sara Stean had ever been *easy* in her life, kept a tactful silence on the subject.

'She's going to be as mad as hell, not to mention really hurt when she finds out you didn't tell her about Mum.'

Despite a shaky start George's only child had always been extremely fond of Hilary who, during her teenage years, had frequently acted as a buffer zone between the warring factions. The trouble was, he reflected wryly, neither George nor Sara was willing to give an inch. They were both stubborn as mules—though Sara was a lot better to look at.

An image of Sara's face with its square little chin, wide, soft mouth and unusual blue-green eyes flashed into Sean's head. He wondered if she'd grown her hair. The last time he'd seen her, her rich auburn-gold mop had been trimmed back to jaw-length bob, but he found he liked to think of it as it had been previously: a silky waterfall that almost reached her waist. Why he liked to think of it at all was something he didn't dwell on…

George's shrug acknowledged Sean's statement. 'You know I can never do anything right as far as that girl is concerned,' he complained.

Tell me about it! Sean thought, running over the events of his last stormy encounter with that impossible young woman in his mind.

He still hadn't figured out why the hell he'd kissed her; it wasn't as if he was attracted to her. *Not much…!* For starters he didn't date twenty-two-year-olds and few things in his eyes could be more high maintenance than having any sort of personal relationship with someone as volatile, spoilt and plain unreasonable as Sara Stean.

Maybe it had been pure frustration—reasonable argument and Sara Stean were not acquainted. Even now it made his jaw tighten just to think about her point-blank refusal to see reason. She'd stormed into his office in the middle of an important meeting and started slagging him off in front of clients. Whatever the motivation behind his ill-judged reaction there was no doubt that her reaction had been way over the top! One thing was for sure—he wasn't going to be doing George any favours where his errant daughter was concerned in the future.

'You know she'll come home if you tell her about Mum.'

'I know, but I was hoping…' George's broad shoulders squared.

'That she'd come home of her own accord…?' Peace in our time seemed a much more realistic scenario to Sean.

'But things have changed.'

'That's what I've been saying…'

'No, I don't mean Hilary.' The burly figure rubbed a hand over his jaw; Sean was concerned to see it tremble. 'Sara's pregnant.'

Sean's own fingers closed around the mother-of-pearl comb he'd been idly toying with from the cluttered dressing table; his knuckles were white. There was a long silence during which George Stean slumped back down onto the bed.

'No, that can't be,' Sean heard himself finally respond with stubborn, uncompromising conviction. He had no idea why he was so sure, he just *knew* that Sara couldn't be pregnant…to be pregnant you needed to…

He shook his dark head and began to pace across the narrow room; his long, loping, tigerish strides took him from one end to the other in twenty seconds flat. He stopped and turned. 'It's just not possible…'

Inside his guts were tied in a tight knot of rejection, which was only natural, he told himself. The girl was almost like a…a…*sister* to him. Sean studiously ignored the wry voice pounding in his skull.

Under the circumstances any man would feel protective…protective as in separating some selfish, careless slob from his head painfully sort of protective.

George lifted his head from his hands and looked up at the tall younger man, who was looking as pale as he felt and even more grim.

'I'm afraid there's no doubt, Sean. They've clocked her coming out of the maternity clinic at St Joseph's on six separate occasions during the past month.'

God! Sean struggled to accept the facts George was presenting him with. For the first time in his life he understood the attraction of burying your head in the sand.

Six! He wasn't exactly au fait with such stuff, but that seemed pretty excessive to him. Was Sara having problems with her pregnancy…? He didn't share his growing suspicions with George—in fact looking at the distraught figure made him realise he'd not exactly been the tower of strength the poor guy had been looking for so far.

What the hell's up with me anyhow…? It's not as if I expected her to stay a virgin for ever. He shrugged pragmatically and forced himself to smile.

'She won't be the first single girl to get pregnant, you know, George. Besides, she could be providing you with that heir you always wanted.' *That would let me off the hook,* he reflected, trying to look on the bright side of the situation. George offering to leave him his empire if he came to work for him was getting to be a biannual event.

George Stean looked perceptively brighter as he considered his stepson's words. Then his face dropped. 'All she needs is a husband now.' He shot his stepson a keen, searching glance.

Sean bit back the scathing retort on his tongue. The sort of man who was stupid and thoughtless enough to get a young woman pregnant was no sort of husband for anyone in his censorious eyes.

'Who,' he asked casually, 'is the father?' His hands, held loosely at his sides, bunched into fists.

'That's the thing, Sean, I've not the faintest idea. The damned agency swears she'd not got a regular boyfriend. She's had dates, of course, quite a few actually, but nobody special.'

A one-night stand or maybe several one-night stands…? You stupid, *stupid* little idiot, Sara! She wouldn't be the first over-protected little girl to go wild when she escaped parental control. Sean faced up to the unpalatable fact it was even possible she didn't know for sure who the father was!

'No surveillance is infallible, George.'

'Well, whoever he is he doesn't seem to be around now.'

Scan greeted this news with frustration. He'd have liked just a few minutes alone with this unknown scumbag.

'Does Mum know?'

'No, I haven't told her yet. The thing is, Scan, I was hoping that you'd…'

'I'd tell her?' Sean prompted as his stepfather, not a man normally at a loss for words, paused uncomfortably. 'If you think it would be better coming from me…?' he agreed doubtfully.

'Actually, it was a bigger ask than that. You know I'm not a narrow-minded man, Sean, but I don't care what anyone says—a child needs a father and a name. A sense of identity and belonging,' he added, warming to his theme.

Sean, who didn't essentially disagree, nodded.

'I can and would give my grandchild anything money can buy…'

'Not if Sara has her way,' Sean predicted drily. My God, there were going to be fireworks. Sara's rejection of her privileged background was total, and as for her stubborn independence, it bordered on the fanatical.

'Sara must never know I had anything to do with it!' George responded, rising to his feet in some agitation.

'Anything to do with what?' Sean, alarmed by his stepfather's high colour and sweaty face, wondered if he'd had his blood pressure taken recently.

Normally he wouldn't consider it his business how a man chose to live his life—he hated well-meaning preachers himself—but George was essential to his mother's well-being. And George never exercised—he smoked, drank and was at least twenty pounds overweight—in fact he could be classed as a prime candidate for a heart attack or stroke.

'The thing is, Sean, I was hoping that you would marry Sara for me, give the baby a name.'

This had to be a joke...*right*? He searched the older man's face but failed to discover any sign of humour.

'You want me to...*what*?'

'I know it sounds a bit...a bit *extreme* when you hear it the first time.' He met his stepson's incredulous grey eyes and shrugged uncomfortably. 'Maybe the second time too, but when you think about it it's not so crazy. You're not in love with anyone else...?'

'I'm thirty-two, George—I've not exactly given up hope yet...' And until then there didn't seem any harm enjoying his freedom. 'Besides, I'm the same man you warned off in no uncertain terms a few years back...?'

The older man flushed. 'That was entirely different, she was young and you...'

'Were not interested, George,' Sean elucidated firmly. 'I was not exactly flattered at the time that you thought I was the sort of sleaze who would make a move on a seventeen-year-old.'

'Well, I'll admit you're not the sort of man I had in mind for her. Not that I'm belittling your achievements...'

'That makes me feel *so* much better about myself.'

His stepson's sarcastic drawl brought a scowl to George Stean's face. 'If she'd gone to university she'd have mixed with a better class of people. People concerned with higher things than making money...'

'But very happy to accept your generosity, which would naturally come at a price.' The older man sent him a look of seething dislike. 'My son-in-law the professor...yeh, I can see that would have a nice ring to it at dinner,' Sean admitted. 'God, what a snob you are, George,' he derided.

'I hate to spoil the fantasy, but your ideas of modern academia are about a hundred years out of date. They are as anxious as everyone else to court the big bucks.'

'Well, that's water under the bridge now. If you must know,' he admitted in a goaded voice, 'I was more worried she'd make a move on you...she threatened as much.'

Sean closed his eyes. 'Let me guess, this conversation took place after you gave her the hands-off lecture. My God, George, what did you expect? If anything can be guaranteed it's Sara walking over the grass when she sees a "keep off" sign.'

'Are you saying that you did...?'

'No, we didn't!' Sean bellowed, losing what little remaining patience he had. 'For God's sake, George, she was winding you up.'

'That's what your mother said at the time,' George admitted ruefully. 'It's just men started looking...and I had such plans for her at the time. It all but broke my heart when she refused that place at Oxford. She's had opportunities that I'd have given my eye-teeth for.'

'I think she was just trying to exert her independence.'

'And look where it's got her!' George cried. 'She needs someone to look after her, Sean, and she won't let me. Look, this marriage wouldn't have to last for ever, but if you marry Sara that will give you some legal rights over the baby. You'll be able to influence the way she brings the child up.'

Sean saw where this was going. 'I'll be able to exert some influence, George, or you will...?'

George Stean's face hardened and Sean got a glimpse of the single-minded ruthlessness that had made the older man a success.

'Have you seen where she's living? The sort of people she mixes with? I'm not having my grandchild dragged up in some slum and his head filled with a lot of New Age nonsense. If I have to fight for custody, prove Sara an unfit mother, I will—I'd prefer not to, of course…'

'*You'd do that?* Drag your own daughter through the courts…?'

George's jaw tightened stubbornly. 'I'll do whatever it takes.'

And with George's legal team, Sean reflected, that wouldn't be too difficult—he had no doubt they could put together a good case against the maternal qualities of a bona fide saint if their client required it—and Sara was no saint. The poor kid wouldn't stand a chance.

'Always supposing I was mad enough to agree…which I'm not,' he added hurriedly, 'what makes you think Sara would marry me?'

'Don't go all modest on me, boy,' George responded jovially, oblivious to the warning signs in the younger man's soft voice and narrowed eyes. 'I've seen the way you work with women.'

'Sara isn't *women.*' No, Sara was a stubborn pain in the neck who just happened to have the sexiest mouth he'd ever seen.

'You won't know until you try…'

'The last time we met,' Sean revealed silkily, 'I kissed her.'

George beamed. 'Excellent! You're halfway there. Your mother always said there was something between you two…'

'The last time it was her knee in my groin…apparently she didn't like being kissed.' Not quite true, but you didn't discuss the moment the girl had started to kiss you back with that girl's father; as for that husky little whimper, you didn't even think about it… Sean made the mistake of ignoring his own stricture and felt lustful flames lick his body—such was the effect Sara Stean had on him.

Sean knew he wasn't the sort of bloke who obsessed

about women, it simply wasn't in his make-up. No, this had to be about the 'what would it have been like?' factor. He sometimes thought it would have been simpler if they'd actually slept together because clearly no sex could be as good as the sex he was imagining!

George winced. 'Well, at least she wasn't indifferent.'

'That's called clutching at straws.'

'You must know your mother has always nursed a secret hope you two would get together,' he hurried on. 'Can you imagine how happy she'd be if you two married…? It would make her last days—'

Sean felt his simmering anger approach boiling point. 'You wouldn't be resorting to a bit of emotional blackmail, would you, George? Because I have to tell you—'

'I'll resort to anything it takes,' came back the blunt response. 'Anything, including giving you control of Stean Holdings.'

'You've made that offer before, George, and I refused.' Sean's own successful production company might not be the global force that Stean Holdings was—but it was his.

'No strings this time.' It was hard to relinquish control, but at least he knew he would be handing the reins over to someone who could handle the job…and God knew there were precious few individuals tough and smart enough to do that!

'You'd have total control the way you wanted…' he continued, smiling confidently. Why wouldn't he be confident? He was quite sure he'd just made an offer that Sean couldn't refuse.

'That's quite a dowry, George…'

As he met the icy grey disdain in his stepson's narrowed eyes he suddenly wasn't so confident. He felt indignant. He'd just made the man the sort of offer that most men would sell their souls for and all the bloke could do was look at him as though he'd just crawled out of the gutter.

'Are you saying no…?' he asked incredulously.

It was only the fact that his mum didn't need the aggro that stopped Sean from allowing his *no* to take a physical form! What was it about the Steans that turned a normally mild-mannered bloke like himself into a Neanderthal…?

'I'm not for sale!'

CHAPTER TWO

SARA approached the door of her tiny flat and turned to say goodnight—not that it had been. It had actually been one of the longest and most tedious ones she could remember, but she was a polite girl. It was at this point she discovered her date, who could have bored for Britain at Olympic level, had brought his large beefy hands to rest strategically on the door either side of her head.

Just what I need, she thought gloomily, anticipating the inevitable undignified tussle. Where does Anna find them? she wondered, considering the dismal stream of losers, of which Ian the beefy rugby player was the latest, her old school friend had set her up with over the last few months. It had reached the stage where even Anna, a girl who considered a single celibate female a challenge, not to mention abnormal, was beginning to lose heart in her pet project.

Maybe I'm too picky?

'You're so beautiful,' her swain slurred, leaning in so close that his broad shoulders totally blocked her view. He was looking down at the outline of her breasts in a lecherous, confident manner. Picky or not, she was not having any of this, she decided, wrinkling her nose in fastidious distaste.

It was clear to her that in his alcohol-soaked mind rejection of his advances was not even a possibility, but then he wasn't one of the brightest creatures she'd ever come across.

His air of cocky confidence was replaced by an expression of truculent ill humour as she nimbly ducked under his arm and placed herself far enough away to escape the fumes from his breath.

'And you're drunk,' she replied factually.

Actually she was amazed he was still standing after the amount he'd consumed over dinner, courtesy of the generosity of Anna's date who had ordered a lot of wine but drank hardly any himself—Anna kept the smart, articulate ones for herself.

'Not *too* drunk, sweetie,' he informed her with a lecherous wink.

Sara was actually more irritated than worried by the turn of events. When it came to looking after herself, if all else failed she had one or two useful and extremely dirty tricks up her sleeve—theoretically at least—that would leave any would-be assailant in pain long enough for her to make good her escape, always supposing she had the stomach to employ them…?

When she later reviewed the events of the next twenty seconds or so she came to the conclusion that overconfidence had been largely responsible for what happened next.

The speed with which he moved for such a big man took her totally by surprise, as did the immense strength of the arms that pinned her own to her sides as she was crushed up against the wall.

The pressure was so great the rough surface of the wall abraded her back through her thin shirt. She hardly registered the pain; her brain was madly racing. She stifled the natural urge to scream blue murder and forced herself to smile flirtatiously up into the flushed face of her captor—it took a great deal of resolution.

'My, you *are* a strong one…' Dredging up unsuspected acting ability from somewhere, she gave a vapid giggle and fluttered her eyelashes wildly.

'Eh…?' he grunted, looking confused but hopeful.

'I do so like a strong man,' she gushed.

Lapping up the admiration, the big man began to look pleased. As he bent forward to nuzzle her exposed neck his grip slackened, not much, but it was enough for Sara's purposes.

Sara didn't waste precious moments enjoying his bewildered expression as he landed flat on his back and lay there gasping like a stranded fish; she headed straight for the door of her flat. Unfortunately her fingers were shaking so much it took her four attempts to insert the key in the lock and turn it. Adrenaline surging through her body, she slipped inside.

Relief, however, turned to horror when, instead of slamming shut, the door hit a large booted foot inserted between it and the door jamb. Despite all her weight pressed against it, the door was steadily pushed open. In slow motion the rug she was standing on slid with her on it backwards across the parquet floor.

Sara's feet seemed stuck to the rucked rug as she watched, dry-throated with trepidation, as her rejected suitor entered the tiny, narrow entrance hall.

That's torn it!

Trying desperately hard not to let her escalating dismay show, Sara raised her chin. Despite the fact she knew that without the element of surprise she didn't stand a chance of physically expelling him, she decided to try and bluff it out.

'Listen, erm…Ian,' she began reasonably. 'I don't want to be forced to hurt you, but…'

Ugly laughter cut in before she could inventively claim black belts in several martial arts. It had been worth a try. She released a tiny, philosophical sigh. So what next, Sara…? Scream…run…? Offer him coffee…? She was hurriedly weighing up her very limited options when a third voice offered a fresh perspective.

'I'd listen to what she's saying if I were you, mate. Imagine the humiliation if it got out that you'd been beaten up by a seven-and-a-half-stone girl.'

It was a deep, slightly lazy drawl that suggested its owner

viewed the world with amused cynicism. A voice that in its own way was as individual as a set of fingerprints. A once-heard-never-forgotten sort of voice—Sara had certainly not managed to forget it, which probably accounted for the fact she didn't feel the rush of relief most people might consider normal in such circumstances. The only rush she felt—much to her extreme horror—was a hormonal one, a primal surge that raised her temperature by several degrees and had a deleterious effect on her ability to think straight.

'Eight stone, and *woman*,' she gritted. She might be a drooling, lustful idiot, but she had no intention of sounding like one! In that at least she was successful; on the other hand nobody paid her any heed—no big surprise here! Aside from the fact Sean *never* listened to her, the two big men were obviously more interested in eyeballing each other than anything she had to say.

This was the closest she'd ever been to having two men fight over her and she didn't feel flattered. Like two dogs after the same bone, me being the bone, she thought, extremely exasperated by this masculine posturing. Except of course the analogy fell down on account of the fact one of them didn't actually want the bone—if he had he wouldn't have let something like a little kick deter him—he just didn't want anyone else to have it!

She edged back against the wall as her second uninvited guest casually peeled his stunningly elegant length off the doorframe he was leaning against. It didn't matter what Sean wore, a designer suit or scruffy jeans—today it was faded denims that clung in all the right places—he always looked mouth-wateringly superb.

She held her breath as he shouldered his way farther into the tiny vestibule. I just hope the lease doesn't make me responsible for structural damage, she thought as the walls started acting as if they were moving inwards…logic told her they weren't, but the illusion was scarily real.

She closed her eyes tight for a moment and took a deep breath. *Better…!*

Now she could view the late-comer with calm objectivity…well, *almost*! Though equally broad across the shoulder and just as tall, unlike the amorous rugby player this new arrival was not muscular in an obviously bulky body-builder way; he had instead a hard, lean, hungry look about him.

Despite his light banter and careless manner, underneath the heavy lids there was a very mean look in his pale grey, densely lashed eyes, a warning that he played tough when he had to…and sometimes when he didn't, just for the hell of it!

'Who the hell are you, and what business is it of yours?'

Under the macho bluster and chest-puffing Sara could tell that her date—evidently not quite so stupid as she'd thought—had picked up on that mean look too.

'I'm the bloke who taught Sara here how to rip losers like you into little bits,' Sean explained modestly.

Under his cool smile there prowled a rage of dramatic proportions. Resorting to physical force should always be the very last resort for a civilised man…he kept reminding himself of this fact at frequent intervals.

'What are you, her brother…?'

'*No!*'

Identical timing and indistinguishable tones of revulsion added extra emphasis to the forceful denial that Sara and Sean both instantaneously made.

'I was only asking! No need to yell…' The effects of the wine were beginning to fade, leaving Ian with an outsized headache and loss of libido. He never had liked redheads—too much attitude.

'I should warn you,' Sean replied, flicking a sideways glance, 'that she's always been enthusiastic on the violence front—nev punches, did you, Sara?'

'It was a reflex,' Sara snapped, her cheeks burning fierily at his snide reference to the mortifying occasion when she'd panicked like some silly, gauche schoolgirl just because he'd kissed her. 'God, if you were my brother I'd emigrate,' she choked.

'If you were my sister I'd buy you the ticket.'

'If you don't leave,' she gritted, 'I'll call the police.'

After considerable reflection—more than she actually liked to admit to—Sara had come to the conclusion that if she hadn't kneed him it would most likely have been an instantly forgettable kiss. Unfortunately the embarrassment factor of her dramatic overreaction had apparently resulted in the incident being indelibly seared into her memory.

What she needed was a man so spectacularly gifted in the kissing department he would erase all memory of that other kiss from her mind; this would be the sort of kiss that could turn her bones to water and her mind to mush.

You wouldn't have thought it would be *that* difficult!

Unfortunately Sara had discovered that bone-melting kisses and men that could administer them were not that easy to find!

Sean flicked her a typically patronising look of dismissal. 'Call whoever you like but shut up for a minute, Sara, there's a good girl.'

Good girl! Sara clenched her teeth and counted to ten. While s͟ ͟ ͟ her eyes slid to the mouth that had ad-
mini͟ ͟ ͟ ͟ ͟gry bone-melting kiss—at least, it had
f͟ ͟ ͟ ͟ ͟so had she; by the end she'd been…not
͟ ͟ ͟n that, Sara!—the implacable firmness
͟ ͟ ͟ ͟o was counterbalanced by a hint of
͟ ͟ ͟fuller, equally shapely lower.
͟ ͟ ͟hree quarters and was still strug-
͟ ͟ ͟at least she supposed the un-
͟ ͟ ͟r limbs and the tightness in
͟ ͟ ͟ger.

Nobody had ever accused her of being an ungrateful person and if it had been anyone else rescuing her from this sticky situation naturally she'd have been grateful, *extremely* grateful.

But it wasn't anyone else, it was Sean, the very last person in the world she wanted to be caught by in a mortifying situation like this. She glared with simmering dislike at his damned near perfect profile. As always there was *something* about Sean, there had been even before the kiss…a combination of *somethings*, actually, that irritated the hell out of her!

For starters his dark, dramatic looks and his charismatic presence naturally gave him an unfair advantage in life, and then there was the fact that, though she was not a short girl—one man had been moved to liken her long limbs to those of a gazelle—she always had to crane her neck to look up at him. But most of all it was his inflexibility, his air of superiority and his total conviction that he was always right—especially as this often proved to be the case.

Admittedly he didn't bluster and bellow like her dad, but the end result was much the same. She'd watched it happen herself. Sean would say something and the people around would immediately start acting like a load of stupid sheep who'd suddenly found a natural leader in their midst.

Natural leader…*ugh*! Definitely a breed Sara couldn't abide.

A leader of sheep would make Sean a ram, she mused. The whimsical analogy struck her as ironic, because if she'd ever pictured Sean as any member of the animal kingdom it had always been a wolf—lean and ruthless with a total lack of humanity… A hazy vagueness drifted across her face as she recalled the impression of whipcord strength she had received when she'd been crushed up tightly against his hard, lean body.

Her eyes glazed over as she recalled the warmth…no, the

heat of his body and the layers of scent on his skin. The light citrus of some expensive-smelling male cologne, the freshly laundered smell of his crisp shirt and, overlying and overlapping everything else, the deeply exciting musky scent of an aroused male. He'd been hot and so had she... Her heart rate slowed and her breathing all but stopped as the prolonged flashback took her over completely.

Then it was gone and she was left light-headed and dizzy, waiting for the wave of paralysing lust to wash over her and pass. It would pass, wouldn't it...?

How was it possible to feel this way about someone you didn't even like? she despaired.

'Don't take that patronising tone with me, Sean Garvey!' she snarled. It had passed; she only had the liquid, squirmy sensation low in her belly to remind her of her weakness. Planting her hands on her hips and pursing her full lips, she glared antagonistically up at him. If *half* the stuff she'd heard about his antics was true, maybe *ram* was more applicable than wolf! 'I'm not one of your unfortunate minions—*thank God*!'

She had been once, for an entire morning—her shortest period of employment to date. The arrangement had come to an abrupt end after she'd chanced to overhear a humiliating conversation that had revealed there actually had been no job and she apparently had been the only one who hadn't known it.

'God, it's so obvious. No way would she have got the job without connections.'

'What job?' had come the laughing reply.

Sara had hidden in the loo until they'd gone. She'd washed away the traces of her angry tears with cold water before she'd marched to his office, silencing his protesting PA with a single haughty look—being George Stean's daughter had taught her that arrogance opened more doors than meek manners.

When she'd confronted him Sean had admitted—with absolutely no trace of shame—that he had created a fictional position as a favour to her worried father, and furthermore he hadn't even been the one paying her salary! Then he'd gone on to suggest she look on it as an opportunity to gain experience in the workplace that nobody else would give her!

'I don't need any favours from you!' she yelled.

'You talk about not wanting any special favours…you want to be accepted, or not, on your own merits.'

'That's right,' she insisted.

'Well, have you ever wondered what would happen to an employee who marched into her boss's office in the middle of an important meeting and demanded his undivided attention?'

Sara's face flamed; pure stubborn pride alone kept her chin at the imperious angle. She had always known that Sean didn't particularly like her, but it wasn't until that moment she appreciated the true extent of his contempt.

'When it comes down to it you'll always be a spoilt little rich girl. You couldn't make it on your own if your life depended on it!'

Sara had barely registered the shocking crack her hand had made as it had connected with his cheek before Sean had taken his retribution by fiercely kissing her.

'I'll second that.'

Sean wasn't likely to forget in a hurry how she'd managed to transform his smoothly run office into anarchic chaos in a couple of hours! As for the distracting effect she'd had on his unsuspecting male employees…!

He would have defended himself vigorously against anyone who might have been rash enough to accuse him of hypocrisy. So he was the one who'd ended up kissing her, under *extreme* provocation; the point was, he hadn't been the only one that had *wanted* to—no, not by a long chalk, he thought sourly, recalling how eager some of the men had been to help the latest recruit learn the ropes.

He supposed he should just be grateful she hadn't turned up for work dressed as she was tonight... His eyes slid of their own volition to the shapely length of her legs. If there had been any visible evidence of her pregnancy it would certainly have shown in that skimpy tight skirt.

He'd come here with the intention of warning her about George's plans to get custody of the baby, but, whilst he still disapproved strongly of the older man's underhand, scummy tactics, it was looking more and more likely with each passing second that her father's concerns were justified. Maybe Sara wasn't up to the demands of being a single parent...?

It was certainly a role that demanded a lot of sacrifices, and *responsibility* definitely wasn't the first thing that sprang to mind when you looked at Sara, but then, he reflected uncomfortably, he couldn't *totally* exclude the possibility that that was his problem...?

One thing that couldn't be disputed was the fact that Sara wasn't letting the pregnancy interfere with her lifestyle, and when her lifestyle included coming home at all hours with drunken thugs like this in tow this couldn't be a good thing for her or the baby.

Maybe she's in denial...? You should know, mate, the ironic voice in his head piped up.

The image he'd seen as he'd rounded that corner flashed uninvited into his head and his lip curled in distaste. Denial or not, someone had to tell her it had to stop... If he hadn't come along when he had, God knew what would have happened—not that she seemed to appreciate the danger she'd been in.

Sara found herself unable to remove her eyes from the pulsing nerve in Sean's lean cheek. Her unblinking scrutiny

did not go unmissed. One of his dark brows rose to a satirical angle as she remained unable to wrench her eyes free.

In defence she blurted out the first thing that came into
her head. 'What's wrong with your face?'

'Nothing, or so I've been told...' The self-derisive light
dancing in his distinctive light eyes robbed his words of
offensiveness.

Sara wasn't mollified.

'Why don't you just go?' she yelled in exasperation. Before you catch onto the fact I'm consumed by lust...if I
carry on like this it can only be a matter of time!

This shrill demand seemed to jolt her sidelined date into
life. He looked from the tall guy with the hostility problem
and the physical presence to back it up to the very angry,
excitable redhead and decided it just wasn't worth the hassle.

'Not exactly a stayer...' Sean mused, observing
Cro-Magnon man's sheepish departure with amused contempt.

'Shut up!' she snarled. 'He may be a total creep but I'd
prefer to spend the evening with him than you!'

'But then that's your taste in men, angel...'

Sara's full lips clamped together. Like I needed reminding
my love life is a disaster area! she thought. 'Who asked
you...?' she ground out, longing to wipe that supercilious
smirk off his face.

'I thought I was a one-off, but it's occurred to me...is
flooring men a mating ritual with you?' So much for acting
as if it never happened, Sean! 'Should I have been flattered?'

'Only if you're insane.' Her voice held an unmistakable
quiver so she paused and took a deep breath. 'As a matter
of fact I abhor violence,' she explained with dignity.

It was hard to maintain that dignified stance in face of
Sean's amused scepticism. She had to admit his scepticism
was understandable. She grimaced, hearing again the hoarse

cry that had emerged from his lips as he'd sunk slowly to his knees...for a horrid moment she'd thought she'd killed him.

'God, what have I done?' she'd cried, dropping to her knees beside him. 'Shall I call an ambulance?'

Sean had refused her offer in the impolitest of terms possible.

'I *do* hate violence!' she insisted now. 'Only sometimes there aren't any viable options.' Screaming 'Take me' to Sean being about as non-viable as you could get. 'It's not *my* fault the world is filled with scummy ratbags.' Her expression of loathing made it quite clear she was looking at the biggest scummy rat of them all. 'What are you doing here anyway, Sean?'

For a week or so after the kissing incident she'd stayed in most evenings and jumped every time the doorbell had rung... It embarrassed her deeply to admit it, but it hadn't seemed totally unfeasible at the time that Sean might have considered the situation unresolved... She'd wondered if he might have wanted to pursue the kissing theme some more.

I must have been deranged!

Well, he hadn't called and she was no longer making the mistake of thinking his presence had anything to do with uncontrolled lust! It was water under the bridge as far as she was concerned; the only regret she had was the fact she hadn't had the opportunity to use her carefully prepared speech—the one that would have left him in no doubt as to her total lack of interest in him in *that* or any other way.

'I'll take your thanks for my timely intervention as read, shall I...?' he suggested drily.

'Thanks? What for?' she puzzled, feigning wide-eyed confusion. 'Oh! I suppose you think you rescued me...?' She laughed. 'I had everything totally under control.' The contention sounded ridiculous even to her own tolerant ears.

Rather than query her version of events, Sean just re-

turned her hostile look with one of gentle, mocking irony
that made her flush. Once her aquamarine eyes were meshed
with his grey ones she found it difficult again to disentangle
them…actually she found it hard to control her breathing
too, which began to fluctuate wildly, causing her small
bosom to do some energetic heaving.

The problem was that she couldn't look at Sean any more
without thinking about that wretched kiss and the glazed
expression she'd seen smouldering hotly in his eyes when
he'd lifted his head just before coming back for seconds.

It hadn't been just that look that had scared her witless,
but the sudden frantic urge to respond to the erotic pressure
of his mouth and the stabbing incursions of his tongue that
had gripped her in the moment before she'd broken free.
Just thinking about it now filled her with shame and made
her stomach muscles quiver with discomfort.

'I see it all now—I interrupted a tender moment…' He
had to make a conscious effort to prevent his eyes from
constantly wandering to her fingers, which were fastening
and unfastening the top button of the bright orange hair-
clashing satin shirt she wore, revealing and concealing in
the process the faintest suggestion of a creamy cleavage.

Sara's slender shoulders sagged and she expelled a noisy,
defeated sigh; it seemed churlish not to admit his arrival had
been fortuitous in one way at least.

'No, you arrived in the nick of time just like the cavalry,'
she admitted. 'Happy now? Or do you want me to grovel?'

His nostrils flared. 'No, but I wouldn't mind knowing
what possessed you to get involved with a total animal like
that,' he snarled.

Sara blinked, taken aback by the depth of his dark, brooding anger.

'And will you stop fidgeting?' he blasted, running an impatient hand through his dark hair.

This grim demand increased Sara's bewilderment. She

followed the direction of his gaze and her hand fell self-consciously away from her throat, leaving her shirt in the revealing mode.

'I wasn't *involved*!'

'Not much...' he muttered. When she waved her arms about like that the orange fabric pulled taut across her chest, revealing the unmistakable outline of her nipples. He was irritated to find his eyes repeatedly straying back to the provocative image.

Sara's expression stiffened at his nasty, sneery tone. 'If you must know it was a blind date...and don't look down your nose at me like that! There's nothing wrong with a blind date...' As if anyone with a track record like his had room for lofty disapproval. 'At least there wasn't until tonight...'

'You mean you've had blind dates before...?'

The incredulous way he said it you'd have thought she'd just admitted to disliking small furry animals.

'Only several hundred...at least, it feels that way.' Her wry smile faded as she encountered the outraged expression on Sean's face. One of his few redeeming features had always been a sense of humour; it would seem he had lost that too.

'You think this is some sort of joke...?' he demanded sternly. 'Don't you realise the risks you're taking for a cheap thrill...?'

Cheap thrill...? His bizarre choice of words was almost as confusing as the outraged parent act he was pulling. *What was his problem...?*

'Does this sort of thing happen often?' he gritted.

'Of course not! Though there was one bloke...'

Sean's stony expression didn't alter but the rhythm of his breathing perceptibly quickened. 'He was violent...?'

His strangled tone brought a frown to her smooth brow. 'No, he was *nice*.'

He scanned her face unblinkingly. 'And nice is a problem...?'

He was trying not to set double standards, but, hell, it was no good asking himself if he'd have been as shocked if Sara had been a male and displaying this attitude to the opposite sex—she quite obviously *wasn't* a male! She was a woman; you only had to look as far as the soft lines of her body revealed in the hair-clashing shirt to see that.

He'd always known Sara had her faults, but if you got past her aggressively independent, stubborn streak and confrontational attitude to life, he'd always thought that her basic strength of character combined with the somewhat extreme set of moral values that old-fashioned school she'd gone to seemed to have stuffed her full of would stand her in good stead... She was the last person in the world he had imagined would display this shockingly careless attitude towards casual sex.

How wrong could a man get...? It was ironic that all these months, while he'd been feeling like a violator of innocence, the *innocent* had been busily working her way through half the male population...!

'Well, *obviously*.' She shot him a reproachful look...did he think she was totally heartless? 'I didn't want to hurt him by saying I wasn't interested in...' She paused and looked up as a strangled sound emerged from Sean's throat.

She wasn't interested in anything that lasted beyond one night as far as he could tell!

'This *nice* guy wanted to see you again.'

'He was very persistent,' she admitted. 'And he was so sweet I couldn't bring myself to say I didn't want anything long term...'

'So what did you do?'

'I told him I was going overseas...'

She looked as if she expected him to applaud her inventiveness.

'A bit drastic...' He found himself feeling sorry for the mug who'd fallen for her.

'Oh, he was *very* keen,' she revealed.

Then, worried she'd come over as pretty hung up on herself, she looked anxiously across at him. She needn't have worried; from Sean's sour expression it seemed to her he was having a hard time imagining *anyone* being keen on her!

For a moment his stuffy condescension made Sara feel like the tongue-tied, insecure teenager with no curves who felt terminally inadequate in the presence of the glamorous and dazzlingly talented stepbrother she saw half a dozen times a year. Happily the feeling didn't last long; she had come a long way since then and not just in the curve department!

'I'm surprised he didn't offer to come with you if he was that smitten.'

Her hand fell away as his antagonistic stare made her aware that she'd started fiddling nervously with the top button of her satiny shirt again.

'To an African village with no running water or telephone...? I'm not stupid, Sean, I didn't make it sound glamorous. The man fancied me, he wasn't ready to commit to a life of selfless sacrifice,' she explained with a self-deprecating grin.

Sean didn't grin back, which was probably a good thing because when those crinkly lines around his eyes deepened...! Boy, *oh, boy*...! She took a deep breath and pulled herself together; not an easy task—even imagining Sean's warm laughter was deeply distracting. Just as well it seemed very unlikely she'd hear it while he was in his present hostile mood.

'And he thought *you* were...?'

'Listen who's talking. If we're talking about life's little luxuries, most people wouldn't consider you're into a

Spartan existence. What car are you driving this week…a Porsche…?' Something sleek and sexy like the women he dated. 'You know what they say about men who drive flashy cars…'

A wicked gleam appeared in his eyes. 'What do they say, Sara…?' Innocence sat very uneasily on his drop-dead gorgeous face.

Sara wasn't daft enough to go there. Especially as post clinch she'd been left with the distinct impression that he didn't have anything to compensate for in the trouser department! Though what did she know? It wasn't as if she were the expert on aroused men.

'You still haven't answered my question,' she reminded him hoarsely. Feeling clumsy—she always had felt clumsy around Sean—she tucked several loose red strands of hair behind her ears. 'What *are* you doing here, Sean?' Other than showing no inclination to kiss me, which might be bad ego-wise but was in every other way a major relief.

Sean's expression grew even more rigid; she sensed rather than saw him taking a deep breath. 'We need to talk, Sara… Shall we go inside?'

Sara moved quickly to block the door into the sitting room. She spread her arms wide as if this gesture could have prevented him going in if he'd wanted to, which it clearly couldn't, she thought, assimilating with a gulp the awesome sum total of his physical attributes—it would take one hell of a lot more than a bit of arm-waving to stop Sean going some place or taking something if he really wanted to…!

She was quite unprepared and therefore helpless to defend herself from the effects of the maverick question that popped uninvited into her head.

And if it were you he wanted to take…Sara…? What would you do then…? Cheeks aflame and less visible parts of her anatomy equally flushed, Sara tore her rapt eyes from his stern and supremely sexy mouth.

There was absolutely no point speculating about something that was never going to happen, she reprimanded herself sternly.

'Not so quick. Did Dad send you…?' He clearly wasn't here for his own pleasure—*hang on to that thought*! 'Are you checking up on me? Or has Dad come up with some new scheme to get me to come home? He's had time; it's been three months since he lost me my job,' she observed bitterly.

'Presumably you got another one.'

'I lost that too.' This time she hadn't needed her father's intervention. The management of the posh French restaurant she had waitressed at had quite unreasonably taken a very dim view of her scheme to give away left-over food, which would have been otherwise binned, to the local homeless population.

'I always suspected you were congenitally unemployable.'

'Well, that's where you're wrong. It turned out very well—I have a job I love now,' she revealed triumphantly. That ought to give him indigestion. 'Somewhere my talents are appreciated.'

Which talents…? 'What are you doing?'

'I work in a bookshop.' The shop, attached to the alternative therapy centre, was a lovely friendly place to work. It had been there she had first become interested in the various therapies on offer at the centre, and acupuncture in particular.

'A bookshop…*you*…!'

His incredulity irritated her. 'Why not me?' she demanded spikily. 'I can read, you know.'

Sean chose discretion and shrugged. 'George doesn't know I'm here…'

Sara recognised evasion when she heard it. 'But he asked

you to come, didn't he?' she demanded. 'Well, you can tell that manipulative control freak from me—!'

Sean's level voice sliced like cold steel through her heated diatribe. 'Mum's ill, Sara.'

Sara froze. *'Hilary…?'* There was nothing much to read in Sean's impassive expression as he nodded, but Sara felt a shiver of unease chase its icy path down her spine. 'Is it…?' she began fearfully.

'It's leukaemia. She could die, Sara,' Sean revealed with bleak lack of expression.

A fractured little hiss issued from her slightly parted lips.

What did you expect, Sean, blurting it out like that? he asked himself scornfully as he watched with growing concern the colour drain from her face, leaving her eyes twin pools of tragic colour in the small, perfectly pale oval.

She evaded the steadying hand he automatically shot out as she swayed. Fending him off with a hands-off gesture, she released a soft moan before abruptly bending forward. The last of her hair grips were shaken free by the jerky action and he watched in unwilling fascination as the shiny copper strands tumbled free, almost brushing the floor as she braced her hands on her thighs and began to greedily gulp air.

'Sara…?'

She didn't act as though she'd heard his voice, rough with anxiety. He touched her shoulder, unsure if his tentative attempt at comfort would be welcome.

Without straightening up Sara brought her hand up across her chest and to cover his where it lay on her shoulder. Not that it did cover it; it was too small in comparison to his own. Smaller and much fairer, he thought, staring at the blue-veined tracery on the back of her narrow hand and her slim, tapering fingers curled tightly over his own.

'I'll be all right, Sean. Just give me a minute…' came the muffled response as her fingers tightened fractionally.

True to her word, it was barely sixty seconds later when she straightened up. She wiped her hand across her damp brow before raising her eyes to his; they glistened with unshed tears. He watched as the fine muscles in her slender throat quivered as she swallowed.

'Don't worry, I'm not going to pass out.' Though that probably had been the nearest she'd ever been to it. *Dear God, why, Hilary...?* She took a deep, steadying breath. 'I can't rule out throwing up, I'm afraid...' she confessed, trying to control her wildly churning, oversensitive stomach.

'Do you do that a lot?'

Sara stared at him blankly.

'Are you sick a lot?' he added slowly.

Sara shook her head, unable to understand his apparent fixation with the subject. Unless he had decided she was bulimic as well as some sort of moral degenerate...!

'It's passed now.'

Had she been suffering bad morning sickness? This would explain why there were no visible signs of pregnancy, he thought, eyeing her slim curves objectively... Normally he had no problem with objectivity—it was one of the things that were responsible for his success—but somehow it eluded him just now.

Even his impartial eyes could see her face seemed to have lost some of its youthful plumpness—the weight loss emphasised the delicate bone structure of her face and made her look older. She's not older though, he reminded himself before he started thinking things he shouldn't be...*as if he weren't already*!

A ten-year gap was totally unacceptable when one half of the equation was only twenty-two. It wasn't actually an age thing, it was more a state of mind. The women he dated were looking for sex and a good time—*like Sara...*? Maybe a trophy boyfriend to show off to their friends...he could deal with that.

What he couldn't deal with, and they didn't need, was constant reassurance. They didn't subject him to emotional tantrums...in short they were predictable. He could fly to the other side of the world if pressure of work demanded he do so without explaining his decisions to anybody. Maybe that made him selfish, but that was the way he liked it.

Sara was by nature demanding, and if he'd needed any proof of her immaturity her behaviour since she'd been living alone was ample proof of it! Then there was the added complication of their tortuous family dynamics. No, whichever way you looked at it, getting involved with Sara remained about as good an idea as swimming in a freezing river at New Year.

CHAPTER THREE

SEAN suddenly realised that some time in the last five minutes he'd made the seamless transition from total denial to admitting he was seriously attracted to Sara, and, though her aggressive attitude might have fooled a less experienced man, Sean knew the attraction wasn't one-sided. This only made it harder to resist the temptation she offered.

If Sara had been aware of his thoughts she might not have accepted so readily the guiding hand Sean offered as he drew her through to the open-plan living area.

'Sit down,' he instructed, tersely attentive as he pushed her down onto a sofa draped in a large bright patchwork quilt.

'I'm...' Sara's teeth were chattering violently, too violently for her to continue. 'Sorry about that,' she managed after a lengthy pause. 'It just came as a shock. I still can't believe it. Hilary is...she's always been so kind to me.' She bit down hard on her quivering lower lip.

'She's a kind person.'

'Are they sure?' She winced and looked at him apologetically. Her heart ached at the bleak pain she glimpsed in his shadowed eyes. She saw other things too—always lean, he'd dropped at least fifteen pounds since she'd last seen him... Why hadn't she noticed that until now? Because you were blinded by guilt and lust is why, she told herself scornfully, and shame washed over her.

He doesn't fancy you, girl, that's what this is all about, so get over it! she told herself. She finally understood why she had found all the men Anna had introduced her to unacceptable...they hadn't been Sean.

It may not be convenient or even wise, but he's hurting and you can't turn your back on someone in that much pain, especially someone who's stood up for you in the past—a fact you've been conveniently forgetting—when he needs help, and by the look of him he's about due some tender loving care!

Forehead creased, she scanned his handsome face with growing concern. Always prominent, his high cheekbones were now even more sharply defined, as if some invisible hand had stretched his olive-toned skin over the slashing curves. The grooves running from his nose to his wide mouth seemed etched deeper and the fine mesh of lines running from the corners of his eyes more noticeable.

He looked liked a man who'd been to hell and still hadn't got back yet.

Compassion for his silent suffering swelled in her chest. His peculiar attitude and strained, tense manner made complete sense now. She cursed her selfishness. If she felt wretched about Hilary, Sean had to feel a million times worse.

'Stupid question, of course they're sure. This must be terrible for you,' she said, wincing at the triteness of her words but taking comfort in the knowledge that whatever she said would sound pretty inadequate.

'Is this you being supportive?' he wondered out loud.

'If you'll let me.' Shyly she let her fingers brush the back of his hand. 'Anything I can do…just say…*anything*!'

Anything had never had more tempting variations. Her sincerity made his crude mental response all the more contemptible.

'I'll let you know.'

The sweep of his dark lashes lay against his cheekbone, hiding his expression from her, but the faint flush just visible beneath his dark complexion suggested her words had embarrassed him. Sean never had been a man given to overt displays of emotion. Satisfied he'd got the message, she lightened her tone to ease his obvious discomfort.

'You know, I always felt secretly envious of your relationship with Hilary.' His expression suggested she'd succeeded in startling him—not an easy thing to do. 'Seeing a non-dysfunctional parent-child relationship up close was actually a bit of a revelation,' she explained with a chuckle. Not that Sean had been a child at the time; after seeing him for the first time she'd gone to her bedroom and taken down the posters of her favourite boy band whom she'd immediately recognised could hardly have competed. 'Up until then I thought a constant state of unarmed combat was the norm.'

Sara had been resisting her father's attempts to control every aspect of her life from a very early age.

'We had our moments—you didn't see me when I was a teenager.' Because she'd barely been weaned at the time— this seemed the moment for a brutal reminder.

Sara, her elbows propped on the sofa arm, rested her chin on her steepled fingers. 'Were you very bad?'

'I liked to think so.'

Sara laughed, imagining a little wistfully the hearts he must have broken at the time.

'Actually I was a closet nerd.'

'Never!' she hooted.

'It's true, I wasn't into team sports, a very important ingredient of coolness, and I preferred messing about on my computer to hanging out with mates and going to rock concerts.'

'But you went along for appearances' sake…?'

'Sure, I did my fair share of bowing to peer pressure,' he conceded.

Sara had a problem with that; no matter how hard she tried, she couldn't see Sean bowing to pressure from anything or anyone.

'Sean...?'

'Yes.'

'How's Dad taking it?'

'It's a hard thing to accept you're going to lose someone you love, Sara, and it's even harder accepting there's not a damned thing you can do about it...' He inhaled deeply and ran both hands through his thick almost-black hair. 'If there was,' he continued drily, 'George would have done it. He's hardly left her side, Sara. He's consulted every expert there is...'

'Don't worry, Sean, I give the devil his due. I know Dad has his good points, and I've never doubted that he loves Hilary.' She smiled and continued thickly, 'It's hard not to love her. The only thing I found hard to believe was her loving him back.' She tried to smile at her weak joke but found she couldn't.

Sean handed her a tissue and she smiled her thanks at him before blowing her nose.

'Is she in hospital?'

'Not now, she's at home. They can't give her any more chemo. Her only hope now is a bone marrow transplant, but they can't find a compatible donor and there's not much time left...'

'How much time?' she whispered.

'Not long.'

Sara released a slow, shuddering breath before her expression firmed.

'Then you must make the most of every second you have with her,' she cried, catching his hand urgently. 'Don't waste a single second and tell her all the things you've never said but meant to, now, while you can. If you don't you'll regret it. Tell me you will, Sean!'

It was only when she paused for breath, her chest heaving, that she recognised the embarrassing fervour of her entreaty. She saw his grey eyes swivel towards her hand locked with his and realised that she had his fingers in a grip so tight her own knuckles were bled of all colour. Unable to meet his eyes, she surreptitiously withdrew her hand—at least it would have been surreptitious if his own fingers hadn't resisted slightly as she'd tried to draw away.

His resistance only lasted seconds, but Sara's heart was thudding against her ribcage and she was ridiculously close to panic by the time she finally succeeded in extricating her hand from his warm grasp. Gazing at it lying on her lap, she began to mumble awkwardly.

'That is, you don't have to, of course…it's just a suggestion…'

'Who didn't you tell, Sara?' Sean lowered himself onto the arm of the sofa and gently tilted her chin up towards him.

Sara's eyes widened, so shocked by the soft question she forgot to avoid staring straight into his eyes; the distinctive silvery paleness stood out in sharp contrast to the dark ring outlining the pupil.

'Your own mother…?' he suggested gently, displaying a spooky ability to read her mind.

Sara began to speak in a low, driven voice; the words spilled from her lips. Some instinct told Sean she was saying things that she had wanted to say for a long time.

'I was ten, they sent me away to boarding-school when she got ill.' She tried to speak matter-of-factly but even now she could recall the bewilderment of suddenly being shipped away from everything that had been familiar.

'That must have been tough.'

Sara's thoughts were so far away she hardly registered the gentle prompt. 'Oh, it was a very nice school, I made lots of friends…' Her brow furrowed a little as she considered her years there. 'But I still felt like being there was some sort of…'

'Punishment…?'

There was shock in her eyes as they flickered to his. 'No…yes…I… They did it to protect me,' she explained, a shade of defensiveness creeping into her voice.

It was deeply unsettling talking to someone who seemed able to walk about in your head, especially when you had a few things hidden away in there you didn't want that person to discover.

'I'm sure they did,' he agreed readily, a dry note in his voice.

The way he saw it, even the best-intentioned parents were only ever an unwary step away from emotionally scarring their children. It was one of the things that made him extremely wary of parenthood, the others being that he enjoyed his freedom and he'd seen too many so-called *perfect* couples split up acrimoniously.

'I didn't even know anything was wrong,' Sara continued, her expression far away. 'The first I knew about it was when Dad came to school to take me to the funeral.'

Sean studied her pale, subdued face; she seemed totally unaware of the heartbreaking image her words painted.

'I always wished I'd had the chance to say goodbye, tell her…' Suddenly she couldn't speak for the emotional lump in her throat. She was startled to feel her eyes fill with tears once more.

The anguish felt so real, so fresh, which was silly—it had happened such a long time ago and Sara didn't believe in living in the past. She supposed that what was happening to Hilary had brought it back.

'I'm sure she knew, Sara.'

His soft voice seemed to bring her back with a jolt from the distant place she'd returned to.

'Don't say anything to Dad, will you?' The wide-spaced green-tinged blue eyes levelled at him were anxious. 'I've never spoken to him about it. He's never liked to talk about Mum. He'd be upset if he knew. He was just trying to protect me.' And he still is, she almost added as Sean continued to look at her in that odd way.

In the few silent seconds that elapsed before his expression lightened a tension materialised out of nowhere; you could almost feel it in the air around them. Sara's ears were filled with the heavy, dull thud of her heartbeat; she wanted to run, run fast enough to release the strange build-up of energy that crackled through her, but she couldn't move. Like someone mesmerised, she stared at his face, fighting a compelling urge to reach out—to touch him...

Even if it did mean he was laughing at her, Sara was mightily relieved when his mobile mouth quirked. Before she could relax properly the brief ironic smile faded, though there was a shade of warm amusement in his eyes as he slid his thumb wonderingly over the gentle curve of her cheek.

'What is it with you Steans?'

'How do you mean...?' It grew increasingly difficult to keep her eyelids open as the feather-light caress continued across the downy smoothness of her face, tracing a line from her chin to her cheekbone and back.

'You can't put the pair of you in a room together without removing all sharp objects as a precaution, and here you are fretting about upsetting him.'

'And you see some conflict in that...?' She grinned and pretended amazement, but inside she was just relieved that he wasn't touching her any more—at least, the sane part was; the other part of her wanted to catch his hand and press her lips against his palm. How would his skin taste...? 'I suppose you have to be a Stean. Or live with one...'

'Is that an invitation, Sara...?'

'Very funny.' She scowled, hoping nothing in her expression would reveal how her wayward imagination was busy providing illustrated examples of what living with Sean would involve! What would he look like in the morning when he woke up...before he woke up?

'Have you ever…?' she was appalled to hear herself blurt out inquisitively.

'Lived with anyone?' He didn't seem put out by the question. 'No, I like my own space.'

And there wasn't much of that here.

No way was it the slum of George's description—in fact the area was tipped by those in the know as somewhere about to experience a major price boom. If the number of Mercedes and Range Rovers parked on the street was any indicator, quite a few of the well-heeled upwardly mobile had already arrived.

Posh neighbours aside, there was still not enough room for the proverbial cat, let alone a baby, Sean thought as he looked around the simply furnished living space. It was neat and cheerful, with some flashes of inspirational colour, but definitely not suitable for bringing a child up in.

He wondered whether Sara had even begun to take on board the practical problems that lay ahead if she didn't swallow her pride and accept George's help.

'Isn't that a bit unusual for someone of your age?' He must be wondering why I can't let the subject drop—hell, I'm wondering myself!

'I'm only ten years older than you.'

She was amused that Sean of all people seemed sensitive on the subject of age…perhaps he had a bit of normal vanity after all. 'I think you might have a few good years in you yet,' she returned drily.

As she looked at his body, all six feet five aggressively masculine inches of it, Sara's teasing smile faded. He had a lot more than a *few*. Even if he hadn't been in superb physical condition—which he was—some men had a sexual appeal that was ageless and she suspected Sean was one of them.

'I'm relieved.'

He didn't look relieved, he looked…what…? Edgy. Yes,

that was the only word she could of think of to describe his manner. It made her nervous, and when she was nervous she chattered.

'Of course, some men of your age who haven't come out of the closet live alone...'

'Or are you inferring I'm gay?'

'Hardly,' she choked, thinking of the women he'd dated—the ones she knew about, anyhow. 'If you hadn't interrupted I was about to say that that left the emotionally immature, afraid-of-commitment type.' Dating a topless model was not the action of a man seeking a life partner...so what if she'd had a degree in economics? Somehow Sara didn't think it was her knowledge of the world markets that had attracted Sean.

'So you're the big expert on men, are you now, Sara?' His eyes lingered on the soft lines of her full lips, presently pressed in a thin, disapproving line.

Sean had never understood men who got hung up about their partners' previous lovers—what did it matter what had happened before they'd come along? Which begged the question...why was he fighting an inexplicable urge to delve into the murky depths of Sara's sex life? A previously untapped masochistic streak...?

They weren't even lovers and never were going to be... Could that thought sound any less resolute?

Sara quenched a prickle of antagonism as she saw him look critically around the room once more. It might not be much compared to what he was used to, but she was proud of the home she'd put together from scratch. She supposed it wasn't realistic to expect someone who lived in an exclusive penthouse apartment to see it that way—to him her tarted-up junk probably seemed just junk.

'You should have seen it before.' Before she'd stripped the grotty floral wallpaper and spent days scrubbing, sanding and varnishing the floorboards. 'Sean...? Do you think I should…?' She began to chew her lip, her eyes not quite making contact with his enquiring gaze.

'I mean, do you think Hilary would mind if I came home…?' She was unable to shake the uneasy suspicion that once she went back her dad would make it damned hard for her to leave again. This wasn't paranoia at work, this was realism.

Sara asking advice from him…? Sara treating him as a trusted confidant… These new developments made Sean pretty uneasy, especially as he was pretty damned sure he couldn't be trusted!

'Or would it be too much of a strain?' she continued fretfully.

'I think you should do what feels right.'

Her smooth brow puckered. 'Is this reverse psychology? I just handed you the perfect opportunity to encourage me to go home. I can only assume…'

Sean shook his head. 'That I was hoping you'd do the opposite of what I suggested.' An incredulous laugh emerged from his throat.

Sara gave a shrug. 'It did cross my mind.'

'Wow, you Steans really aren't big on accepting things at face value, are you?'

'Well, I've noticed that people are usually nice when they want something.'

'Such cynicism in one so young.'

'Listen who's talking!' she retorted.

'Fair point. The only problem with your theory is I didn't actually tell you what to do.'

She pulled a face. 'That threw me,' she admitted with a rueful grin. 'Actually,' she confided with a deep sigh, 'I kind of was hoping you would tell me what to do.'

'What, and take the flak the next time George winds you up?'

'That was the general idea.'

'Do I look that stupid?'

Her lips twitched. 'Can I plead the fifth...?'

'Nice try, but wrong country, angel.' His teasing expression sobered. 'Here any omission is treated as a sign of guilt.'

Just looking at him made her feel guilty.

His eyes narrowed on her troubled face. 'For what it's worth,' he began in an offhand manner, 'I think that if you do go back you should keep on this place...if only to have somewhere to go when you need a break.'

'From Dad?' The sombre expression on his face made her tentative smile fade abruptly.

'With the best will in the world, it's hard living with someone who's dying, take my word for it.'

'You're staying at Springhurst?' she exclaimed.

This was not a possibility that had occurred to her, but of course it made sense Sean would want to be with his mother.

His long-lashed grey eyes sought hers and held them; the tension in him was palpable. 'Does that influence your decision?'

Just the velvet rasp of his deep voice made Sara's stomach flip over; the things he *wasn't* saying, the silent, intimate message in his spectacular eyes made her dizzy and a little breathless...all right, a *lot* breathless. She just hoped she was reading that message right because if not she was about to make the biggest fool of herself ever!

Still on the sofa, she pulled herself up until she was kneeling on the lumpy, uneven surface—the sofa was very second-hand. She still couldn't look him in the eye but she was closer.

'Well, I suppose it might be handy.' She didn't even try and dim the longing in her eyes as she gazed up at him. It was all there for him to see.

Sean drew a harsh breath. 'In case I want that emotional support you offered...?'

She almost heard the silent boom of her pent-up longing breaking through the last barrier. 'In case you want me,' she corrected huskily.

Her eyes widened before shutting tight. Oh, my God, I just made an indecent proposal! I can take anything but not laughter; please, *please* don't let him laugh in my face, she prayed.

Several seconds passed and he didn't laugh; the only sound she could hear was the audible rasp of his laboured breathing.

'Is this seduction inspired by compassion, Sara?'

Her eyes shot open at the husky question. 'No! Oh, no, definitely not. This is lust, mad, bad insatiable lust,' she explained to him forcefully.

Just the way he liked it, in fact, a meeting of appetites not minds...so why was he feeling this nagging sense of dissatisfaction?

Oh, my God, she despaired as her tongue continued to run away from her, what was wrong with a simple *no*...?

'I've been totally consumed by it since you kissed me.' She stopped and, looking into his frozen face, gave a snort of impatience...sometimes words were simply inadequate.

Part of her, a kind of out-of-body Sara, seemed to be watching what she did as she stretched up to boldly place her hands at the back of Sean's head before yanking it down.

She proceeded to kiss the pulse point at the base of his throat and licked her way up the strong curve—how had she known that would be a satisfying thing to do?—until she reached his square chin. She then kissed the slight indentation there. From here she slowly progressed to his lean cheek; after each contact she lifted her lashes and met his eyes. They burnt, like the hot spot you saw deep in the very centre of a flame; it fuelled her ever-increasing sense of recklessness.

Her out-of-body self watched these shameless antics with disbelief.

Sean's contribution remained not telling her to stop, that and the way he was looking at her—no man had ever looked at Sara that way. She had never *imagined* a man looking at her that way!

His big body screamed with tension, she could almost taste it; she *could* taste his skin and that she liked a lot.

She was a whisper away from his sexy mouth when his fingers suddenly pushed into her thick hair. With a muttered imprecation he yanked her head back, exposing the curve of her vulnerable neck.

His nose slid down the side of hers, so close their breath mingled. Dizzy anticipation fizzed right down to her curling toes, and she gave a voluptuous sigh.

'You want kisses…?' he demanded thickly.

No way was he going to go through with George's crazy scheme, but if they were lovers and he was around for a while he could look out for her—*what a saint you are, Garvey!*

Sara shook her head languidly. Hungrily she examined the sensual contours of his mouth.

'Yours,' she admitted shamelessly.

Tonight, she wanted him tonight. This was no exclusivity deal she was talking here. Tomorrow she might want someone else… Sara seemed to have no inhibitions about taking what she wanted; in fact she seemed to have no inhibitions full stop.

'God, I must be mad!' he grated despairingly as he hungrily examined the delicate flush on her passion-tinted skin and the almost feral glow in her lovely eyes. 'But, God help me, you're so damned beautiful. I haven't been able to stop thinking about you.'

Sean just called me beautiful! Sara had not had time to gloat over this extraordinary circumstance before his mouth came crashing down on hers; at that precise moment she stopped thinking and began *feeling*!

It was several minutes before Sean, who prided himself on his control, had regained enough of it to stop kissing her with a bruising, brutal lack of restraint. Not that Sara had seemed to mind. The drumming in his skull got so loud he could feel the echo of it vibrating through his entire body as he recalled the way her soft, pliant body responded to his every touch; it had been like holding a live flame in his arms.

He inhaled deeply through flared nostrils and let her slide back down onto the sofa proper from where he'd bodily hauled her. 'Sorry…'

About what? Sara wondered, opening her glazed eyes. She'd been kissed before, very nicely kissed actually, but never with anything approaching the raw, driving urgency Sean displayed. Never with such *need*, she thought, staring wonderingly into his face. She discovered he looked pretty grim for someone who'd just given any indication of enjoying himself.

Her eyes slid in the direction of the graphic evidence of his pleasure. She managed to pull them back before it became too obvious what she was doing—staring at a man's crotch is what you're doing…? She blushed, afraid he would think her hopelessly crude and vulgar.

'Give me your hand, Sara!'

Without thinking she responded to the soft command.

'Oh, my!' she gasped as he fed her fingers onto his body before letting go. A bolt of sexual longing lanced through her as she felt his erection, confined by the constriction of his clothing, pulse against the light pressure of her palm. She didn't move.

'Don't be afraid to look or touch.' Unable to speak, Sara

nodded. 'I've made your mouth bleed.' His breath whispered fragrantly against her skin as his tongue touched the pinprick of blood near the corner of her mouth. Sara sucked in her breath sharply as an erotic shudder shook her body.

'Don't be sorry. I think I like you a little bit out of control,' she confided huskily.

'How about a lot out of control?'

She shivered. 'That sounds a little scary.' And deeply exciting.

Frowning, he took her face between his hands. 'I scare you?'

'The only thing that scares me is the idea you won't carry on kissing me, Sean.'

His lips twisted into a thin, self-derisive smile. The fact alone that she was carrying another man's child ought to have put her off limits.

'No chance of that,' he rasped. 'I've wanted to do this ever since the last time.'

Sara's sharp gasp of pleasure faded abruptly.

He might have been thinking about her lips, but it had been other women's lips he'd been kissing. It would be totally irrational to feel jealous of those women—or maybe one special one?—who had experienced the pleasure of Sean's kisses during those months. I must have a deeply irrational streak, she decided as a sharp stab of jealousy knifed through her.

'I suppose you were thinking of me while you were kissing the others?'

'There haven't been any.' Celibacy hadn't been a choice—or had it…? He instantly dismissed the absurd notion that kissing Sara and his unusually lengthy spell of abstinence were in any way connected.

It had simply been a string of circumstances.

Firstly the woman he'd been seeing at the time had grown tired of his inattention. Their parting had not been acrimonious and he'd not felt any pangs when he'd heard a little later that she'd found someone else...no doubt someone with less pressure of work. Then, after his mother's illness had been diagnosed, his sex life had not been a priority. So what has changed, Sean...? he asked himself.

Sara.

'None...?'

'I've had other things on my mind.'

'Of course you did,' she replied huskily. She caught his hand, but had no opportunity to display her support further because he chose that particular moment to demonstrate his willingness to carry on kissing her for ever.

His hot mouth was still attached to hers as he pushed her down onto the sofa. Lying underneath him felt even better than she'd imagined it would—and she had imagined, especially late at night in her lonely bed.

She ran her hands over his shoulders, luxuriating in the rippling strength of his powerful, bunched muscles. She was vaguely conscious of his own hands sliding under her shirt to make skin contact. All the muscles in her abdomen contracted simultaneously and she gasped, then pushed her face into his shoulder as his fingers skimmed lightly the surface of her abdomen.

He rolled a little way off her but only to give himself further access to the firm, silky flesh. Anxious to retain as much contact as possible, Sara looped her leg across his waist to anchor herself more firmly to his side but still allow him the freedom to explore further.

Sean took full advantage of that freedom to slide his fingers under the waistband of her skirt. This done, he freed her shirt, which he proceeded to open, exposing her hot skin to the cooling air.

It was relatively easy while touching her smooth, satiny skin to blank out the knowledge that she was carrying another man's child. It wouldn't be as easy when it started to show. Being a father, the sleepless nights, the dirty nappies and, most of all, the overwhelming responsibility had to be hard enough when the baby was yours. When it was not even yours...now that required something altogether more in every way. That would require love.

Dear God, his touch was fire!

'I'm going to make you forget every other man you've ever been with,' he promised.

'That makes you smile...?' He caught his breath, the flare of anger fading from his eyes as he unclipped the front fastening on her bra. Her breasts were fuller than her slender, narrow-backed figure suggested. He breathed in raggedly as he watched her already distended nipples swell to hard peaks before his eyes. He planned to taste those delectable buds; he planned to run his tongue over them until they glistened and then he'd draw them into his mouth. Anticipation made the ache in his groin almost unbearable.

'I was just thinking,' she said, throwing an arm over her head languidly—her every gesture oozed sizzling sexuality as she gazed up at him, 'that forgetting shouldn't be too hard.' Her back arched as he licked his forefinger and ran it around the rosy aureole of her left breast. Then even more shockingly he took her own hand and curved it over the same aching mound.

'See how perfect you feel.'

His throaty, erotic whisper made the strength rush from her body. 'Oh, my God!' she moaned. 'Actually, I'd prefer to feel you.'

'And you shall...*soon*,' he promised throatily.

Sara watched through half-opened eyes as he peeled off his shirt, impatiently pulling it over his head still buttoned. He was so beautiful, it brought a rush of emotional tears to her eyes. There wasn't an ounce of surplus flesh on his tightly muscled torso. His shoulders were broad and there was a light dusting of dark body hair over his even-toned golden skin, though a sliver of paler flesh just above the waistband of his jeans suggested he wasn't quite this dark all over. The thought of things yet to be revealed made her cheeks burn with anticipation.

He threw his shirt to the other side of the room. 'You still don't think I can make you forget your other men...?' he challenged, leaning over her supine figure.

He took her breath away. How did I get this lucky...? she wondered. 'There haven't been any other men, silly,' she crooned lovingly.

Sean stiffened and drew back.

'*Meaning...?*'

His odd manner brought a concerned frown to her smooth brow. 'Meaning you're my first,' she revealed awkwardly.

'Are you telling me you're a virgin...?'

You didn't have to be particularly intuitive to see the idea wasn't a big hit with him. Just her luck if he turned out to have some major hang-ups about virgins!

CHAPTER FOUR

'Is THAT a problem?'

Sean laughed—not a nice sound, and the distant sound of alarm bells began to ring in Sara's head. 'It wouldn't be if I didn't know.' This wasn't strictly true.

'Know...?' Apparently she was meant to know what his cold, cryptic comment meant...?

Sean didn't reply; he didn't trust himself to. It was all that innocent bewilderment she was effortlessly exuding that really got him. Some *virgin*—she'd probably had more lovers than...than what, Sean...? an irritating voice in his head asked. More than you, maybe?

Impatiently he silenced the irritating voice in his head. This wasn't about double standards, this was about blatant dishonesty. Hell, it wasn't as if he was some puritanical zealot, he could overlook the odd white lie, but pretending to be a virgin!

It was sick!

Maybe some of her lovers got an extra thrill from imagining themselves seducing some innocent; personally it wasn't a responsibility he had ever desired.

Sara watched him retrieve his shirt, fascinated even at this worrying moment by the lithe animal grace—*angry* animal at this moment—of his movements.

'What are you doing?'

'Leaving.' He ought never to have come.

'What?' Those bells suddenly got very loud.

'You heard me.'

His inexplicable coldness was like a slap in the face. Totally bewildered by the strength and abruptness of his rejec-

56

tion, Sara tried to sit up. Her actions were hampered by her shirt, which had slipped down her arms. Impatiently she tore her arms free and levered herself into a sitting position. She was shaking. Her unfulfilled body, given a glimpse of what could be, ached unbearably…it was like an all-over tooth-ache.

Was she meant to sit here and watch him go…act as if it didn't matter…? That would be the dignified thing to do.

'You can't!' she wailed.

To hell with pride, she was hurting!

'Watch me.'

Indignation flared in her tight chest. 'I didn't do it delib-erately. Or if you want to be pedantic…*not* do it.' She looked across into his eyes and saw no answering humour, just savage contempt that seemed way out of proportion with her crime…if lack of experience could be considered such.

'For God's sake, Sara, cut out the sweet innocent act!' he snarled. 'I know about the baby!'

'*Baby…?*' She drew her knees protectively up to her chest and rocked forward. She was aware that everything was going wrong without having the faintest idea what had changed. There had to be something she was missing; surely this couldn't be about him being her first lover…?

Sean looked into her wide, confused eyes and couldn't detect anything but innocent bewilderment. His teeth grated together as his jaw tightened. Her ability to fake it so suc-cessfully made him wonder bitterly whether it had all been an act…the emotion, the passion…? Hell, no, that at least had been real, nobody was *that* good at faking it! So hope-fully she felt as bloody awful as he did!

'I know you're pregnant, Sara. Your father told me. In fact,' he revealed with a hard laugh, 'he wanted me to marry you…'

'M-marry…!' This was madness, some surreal dream from which she'd wake up at any moment.

'Temporarily, of course.'

'You really think I'm *pregnant*?' Oblivious to her half-naked state, she leapt off the sofa in one lithe bound and was on her feet managing, despite naked breasts and a skirt that had slipped way down her hips, to look dauntingly dignified.

He spelt it out. 'I *know* you're pregnant.'

Still she shook her head; her denial in the face of his disclosure only increased his growing distaste. Maybe she was too in character to drop the *ingénue* persona straight off…? Very likely some convincing fairy tale was being spun in that pretty head even now.

'You *can't* know.'

Sean misunderstood her fierce contradiction.

'Your father has had you under surveillance—the grubby raincoat brigade…? Surely you didn't think he wouldn't keep tabs on you…?'

'Actually I tried not to think about it.' It had been that or live her life constantly looking over her shoulder. If she'd gone down that road she might just as well have stayed at home. '*Dad* told you. He actually said I'm pregnant…?' She tried to sift the information slowly filtering into her stunned mind.

Sean, his colour heightened, tore his eyes angrily away from the gentle sway of her breasts. He knew he only had himself to blame for being disillusioned.

This was what happened when you took people at face value. This was what happened when you believed what you wanted for the simple reason if you didn't you'd have had to face the unpalatable fact you weren't thinking at all above the waist. What the hell had he thought he'd been doing, making love to *Sara*…?

'If you wanted to keep it a secret, perhaps you should

have slipped into the maternity clinic through the back door.'

Sara released an incredulous gasp; her head came up with a snap. So that was it.

'What the hell are you laughing at?' Sean watched with growing angry resentment as she walked past him and across to the opposite side of the room, her shoulders shaking with the same laughter that fell musically from her lips. Halfway there she stepped out of the skirt and kicked it away; her minuscule pants were hot pink.

Unlike your average *virgin* she didn't act self-consciously about her almost nakedness—not that he knew many virgins…actually, he knew fewer than that. His cynical sneer became a pained grimace as he greedily drank in the details: her legs were slender and long in comparison to her height and her taut bottom was nicely rounded. Above the flare of her hips her waist was very tiny, the skin on her back looked soft and peachy…

'God, your back…! What the hell have you done?' he demanded, staring at the grazed, bleeding area just below her right shoulder blade.

Hand on her shoulder, Sara tried to twist to see the damage Sean spoke of; unable to do so, she lost interest. 'I expect it happened when he pushed me against the wall,' she observed matter-of-factly.

'He…' Sean blinked to clear the red mist that obscured his vision. 'Why the hell didn't you tell me he hurt you…?'

'Hardly hurt; besides, I forgot.' I forgot everything the second you walked in.

'You *forgot*…! Don't you have even the most rudimentary instincts of self-preservation?' he railed.

If I had you wouldn't be here, she thought bitterly. Blotting the dampness on her face with the back of her hand—she wouldn't let him see her crying—she turned around, an expression of lofty disdain on her rigid features.

'That graze needs cleaning.' Sean inhaled deeply and broke out in a cold sweat before he managed to tear his eyes off the thrusting outline of her pouting breasts. It was patently pointless to pretend, considering the rampant response of his body to this display—he didn't doubt for a second that the provocation was callously premeditated—that knowledge of her duplicity had made her any less dangerously desirable to him.

He made a grim resolution to rise above his baser instincts...he wouldn't give her the satisfaction!

'Don't worry, I'll be showering to wash the smell of you off me.' She smiled with grim satisfaction as two stripes of dark colour appeared on the crest of his sculpted cheekbones. 'So you know I'm pregnant...?' Actually she was amazed she could sound so calm when inside she was a seething mass of hurt and anger. 'What a relief!' she sighed sarcastically.

When she thought of them plotting...her hands balled into tight fists. The news about Hilary had evidently just been a convenient way to break down her defences; if not, why had he waited until now to tell her? Only a callous monster would be capable of such a monstrous act. The sort of monster who could come here with the cold-blooded intention of seducing her!

And I thought Dad was ruthless! What a team they make. And you fell for it—*and him*! A wave of self-disgust washed over her when she reviewed her eagerness—only an exceptionally stupid fish threaded the very hook that caught it! Talk about easy money!

Sean slid his arm back into his shirt and shrugged it across his shoulders. Sara swallowed as the muscles low in her belly tightened as she watched the play of fine muscle under his smooth, tanned skin.

'You really do think I'm pregnant...?' Part of her stubbornly persisted in believing this was actually some silly misunderstanding.

'I told you.' Dark head bent, he continued to button his shirt. 'For God's sake, put on some clothes,' he growled without looking at her.

Sara, who had almost forgotten her state of undress, defiantly struck the most provocative pose she could think of—which, given her lack of experience, she feared was probably pretty tame—and eyed him with malicious contempt.

One feathered brow rose. 'What's wrong, Sean? Does my body bother you?' she taunted, letting her fingertips trail suggestively over her smooth, pale skin. She watched the resulting dark stain travel up his neck with intense satisfaction—it was the reaction she'd been hoping for. Sizzling anger bubbled through her; God, but he deserved to sweat!

And sweat he did. There was a sheen of moisture over his bronzed skin when he eventually turned his head. 'You damn well know it does!' he grated thickly.

With a provocative swing of her hips, Sara took several steps towards him. *'Tough!'* she spat, her sweet smile belied by the blaze of suppressed fury burning in her eyes.

His nostrils flared as the scent of her skin drifted towards him.

'Have your fun if you must, Sara.' His cold eyes flicked over her with total contempt. 'But don't try telling me you're not as frustrated as I am right now.'

And then some. Sara gulped, but refused to respond to his challenge. How could she when it was a claim that was well nigh impossible to refute?

'Did Dad happen to mention what sex the baby is?' She pushed a hank of hair out of her eye. 'Or didn't he manage to get an actual copy of my medical records? Incidentally, how far gone am I? I understand the first trimester can be hell. You know, I really should start taking care of myself…let me make a note of that…'

'What's the point in this, Sara?' Sean asked, pushing his shirt back into his trousers before regarding her with weary distaste.

You'll find out soon enough, you treacherous rat.

'So he wanted you to marry me, did he…?' She was so consumed by anger and the sense of betrayal that she could hardly form the shaking words by this point. 'And what did you get for making this supreme sacrifice? I take it you weren't doing it out of the goodness of your heart?'

'If I marry you George will give me control of Stean Holdings.'

The shock of his calm declaration was so great that Sara forgot to maintain her pose of condescending scorn. *'The whole thing…?'* That would be a massive incentive to anyone who didn't have a scruple to his name—it would seem that Sean could be safely placed in that category.

'Total control.'

And Sean liked control.

'My…that must equate to quite a lot of *camels*!' Her laugh was tinged with the hysteria she was struggling to keep in check. 'I'm curious, did you bargain…? Dad offers the publishing side and you say no way, so he comes in with the TV network? Is that the way it works? Until he throws enough into the pot, as in *everything*, to make you overlook the fact you'd have to pretend another man's child was yours. I suppose,' she mused faintly, 'Stean Holdings, would be worth quite a lot of overlooking.'

'Some people might think so,' Sean drawled.

Not only did he not want the damned firm, if it weren't for his mother he'd cross to the other side of the street if he saw anyone with that damned name walking towards him.

You'd have thought I'd have learnt my lesson after

George suckered me the last time. Yep, I should have followed first instincts and let them get on with it, but, no, my sense of justice was so aroused by George's threats that I hot-footed it here like some crusading fool.

'I'm coming home,' she said, making an abrupt decision. Cold grey eyes clashed with stormy aquamarine. 'Because I want to be with Hilary, and I'll even be pleasant to you in front of her.' My God, but that was going to be a big ask. 'But if you so much as touch me…'

Sean, who was making his way towards the door, paused. He gave a thin, sardonic smile. 'I think I might be able to restrain myself.'

She might make him eat his words just for the fun of it, she decided vengefully.

'By the way,' she called out. 'If you see Dad before I do, tell him not to organise the baby shower just yet. You see, I'm not pregnant.'

'Denial isn't going to work when you've got a belly the size of a house.' Something in her face made him pause, his eyes narrowed suspiciously. 'Has something happened to the baby? Or did you have an abortion?' Why had this obvious possibility not occurred to him?

Because despite every evidence to the contrary you carry about this ridiculous idealised mental image of her as a sweet little kid, you dope!

'Tell me, Sean, do you lie awake at nights thinking up ways of insulting me?' she quivered wrathfully.

No, I lie awake at night feeling like a teenager for fantasising about introducing you to the pleasures of sex. Now *that* was ironic.

'When are you going to get it into your thick skull I am not now and never was pregnant?' she bellowed.

From his expression it was clear he was never going to believe her, even if she yelled herself hoarse.

'The hospital Dad's spies saw me going into has a very

open-minded consultant obstetrician,' she began quietly. 'He's very into complimentary medicine and he's just started running a trial scheme offering acupuncture for pain relief during childbirth.'

'Very interesting…'

Sara refused to let his bored drawl put her off. 'He invited me to sit in on some of the clinic sessions with interested parents-to-be and several of the actual deliveries.' That had been an incredible experience.

'Why the hell would he do that?'

She could see a hint of uncertainty mingled with disbelief in his wary scrutiny.

'He'd do that because he's a very nice man, and he knows I want to do an acupuncture course when I've saved up enough money.' That was not going to be for some time on the amount the bookshop paid her. Maybe I should let Dad pay for it—he definitely owes me after this little debacle, she thought grimly.

Sean listened to her explanation in silence. When she'd finished his eyes shifted from her face to a point somewhere over her head. He swallowed. Her words had the definite ring of authenticity about them…besides, who could think up such an unlikely explanation?

'You're not actually pregnant?'

'My, aren't you the quick one?'

His stunned shock was everything she'd hoped for and more, but for some reason she didn't experience the degree of satisfaction she'd anticipated.

'But George said…'

'He said and you believed, so don't try and pass the buck on this one, Sean, because it won't work.'

If he accepted he'd been wrong about the baby, then… He took a deep, startled breath. 'Then you're in fact…' His eyes moved incredulously over her slim, supple body, a body that even now excited a lustful…

'A virgin…yes.' And very likely to stay that way for the foreseeable future after this experience!

'But the men…!'

His indignant tone suggested he'd been the innocent victim of some sort of deliberate deception on her part.

'I think Dad should seriously consider changing his surveillance team…or did you draw your own conclusions, Sean? Are my many lovers a personal touch of your own?' Their eyes met and she gasped. 'It was, wasn't it? That would be right—you never did have much of an opinion of me, did you, Sean?' she breathed bitterly.

'Well, you must admit it's much more likely you'd had your share of one-night stands than you being a…a…'

'Virgin,' she supplied sweetly. He really did have a hard time saying the word. 'Actually, I suppose I have you to thank for that. Though I have to admit I find your massive display of moral outrage a wee bit rich coming from someone who is willing to lie his way into somebody's bed for the sake of a dowry. God, Dad must be really desperate to marry me off.'

'I told him that I wouldn't marry you.'

Gosh, that made her feel better!

'I started to make love to you because I wanted to,' he gritted slowly.

You thought I was pregnant!' she yelled.

'Yes.'

'And that wasn't a problem for you…?' If there was ever a man she couldn't see bringing up another man's child, it was Sean.

'It was a problem,' he admitted. 'But there wasn't much I could do about it.' Other than go slowly mad thinking about the man who she'd allowed to use her. 'I thought you might need someone around for a while.'

'Sure you *and* Saints are like that.' She linked her little fingers tightly together and waved them under his nose. 'In fact you taught them all they know about selfless sacrifice.' Her head fell back. She took several deep breaths before trusting herself to speak again. 'Pardon me while I fall about laughing,' she requested, displaying no immediate signs of mirth. 'You must think I'm an idiot. You,' she declared with loathing, 'are nothing but an opportunist, lying hypocrite!'

The dark lashes lifted off his extraordinary eyes. 'You want me to go…?'

'I want you to go bald before your next birthday.' She regarded his lush dark hair viciously. It was a measure of her wilful stupidity that even at this moment she couldn't help wanting to sink her fingers into the rich waves. 'But failing that going would be good,' she declared coldly. 'What did you think…I was going to invite you to stay the night…?'

His eyes darkened as a strangled laugh emerged from her trembling lips.

'That I'm daft enough to say, *No hard feelings, Sean.* And, *Where were we…?'*

Her teary eyes moved to the sofa, which was a very bad idea. Her treacherous body ached as she recalled exactly where they'd been! A heat spread from the aching area between her thighs to the rest of her body as her breathing got progressively more rapid.

'On the brink of something pretty special…?'

His astonishing words made her spin back. She pulled the back of her hand angrily across her eyes.

'You never give up, do you? When I sleep with a man, Sean, I'd prefer it to be one who isn't being paid for it.'

His head reared back as if she'd struck him. 'If that's the way you want it,' he said in a cold, distant voice, 'I'll say goodnight.'

When the door closed with finality behind him she sank cross-legged to the floor. *Goodnight!* Never had the words been less appropriate; this was the very worst night of her life.

Oh, God, I'm going to be living under the same roof as him! The sheer awfulness of this...the even worse awareness of wanting someone who was a despicable rat both hit her.

It took her several seconds to locate and identify the strident sound that interrupted her orgy of misery. Sean's mobile was on the floor where it had fallen out of his pocket. It stopped ringing just when she was wondering whether she ought to answer it.

It started again the moment she turned away.

Reluctantly she picked it up.

'Hello, darling, it's me,' the low, dramatically husky voice the other end purred. 'Hello. The most *fantastic* news...I've already got the champagne on ice.' Sara wondered if she would make it to the bathroom before she threw up. 'Guess what's happened? No, don't, I'll give you a clue. Right at this moment I'm wearing...'

The knowledge she was about to hear something she definitely didn't want to aroused Sara from her state of catatonic shock...though why she should be shocked because Sean received calls from women with sexy voices who wanted to tell him what they were or weren't wearing, she didn't know.

'Sean isn't here,' she blurted out abruptly.

'Oh, what a nuisance. Have you any idea where I might be able to make contact? It's actually quite important...'

'I could tell,' Sara choked bitterly. 'Who shall I say was calling?' a morbid curiosity impelled her to ask.

'Oh, he'll know who it was,' came the confident reply.

'Actually,' Sara admitted grimly, 'I've no idea where he is and I couldn't care less!' To think I swallowed that corny line about him not having kissed a woman since me—sure, that was *really* likely, Sara.

After hanging up she went into the kitchen, filled the sink with water and ritually submerged the slim phone in it.

Sean had been aware of the figure standing in the shadows even before he revealed himself.

'Bad timing, George,' he gritted.

'I just thought I'd get a progress report. How is our little plan proceeding—going well?'

His stepson turned and fixed him with an unwavering glare that would have had nine out of ten men seriously worried—with good reason.

George Stean was not a sensitive man.

'Ah, *that* bad!' He clicked his tongue sympathetically.

Sean's fists clenched. 'For starters, George, there is no plan.'

'That could be your mistake, my boy. I hope you don't mind me giving you a little piece of advice...'

'Yes, as a matter of fact I mind very much.'

The venom in the younger man's tone clearly took George aback momentarily. 'There's no need to be so touchy. It's just I know Sara, there's a knack to handling her.'

'Oh, really...?' Sean raised a brow—it was a real struggle to contain his temper. 'Remind me...when was the last time you saw or spoke to her?'

A dark, angry colour suffused the older man's sagging cheeks.

'Does it ever occur to you,' Sean demanded harshly, 'that Sara doesn't want to be handled, she doesn't want to be manipulated like a stock price? She just wants to be treated with the respect you'd afford anyone else and maybe loved in an unconditional, no-strings-attached way.'

'How do you mean exactly...?'

Sean gritted his teeth and shook his head in disbelief. 'You've not the *faintest* idea, have you? I'm beginning to think that Sara knew what she was doing when she left home. Your problem is you still think of her as a child...'

George suddenly had a revolutionary idea. It was so off the wall that he was inclined to dismiss it straight off...then he looked at Sean's face. 'Are you sure it's *me* we're talking about here?'

Sean froze, an expression of shock filtering into his eyes. Then, with a curse and a last snarling glare at George, he wrenched open his bedroom door and then slammed it with equal vigour behind him.

CHAPTER FIVE

SARA stepped into the hallway, her trainers silent on the polished stone floor.

It had taken her the morning to sort things out.

Rupert in the upstairs flat wasn't back from his Vancouver trip until that evening, so she had left a note apologising for killing two of his pot plants in his absence—two more looked terminal to her. She begged him to overlook this horticultural homicide and hoped he wouldn't mind feeding the stray cat that had adopted her. A mangy creature, not given to overt displays of affection, it had somehow wormed its way into her affections.

A week, she'd explained to Amber at work, should be enough for her to gauge the situation. She would be extremely sorry if it turned out she had to hand in her notice, but she felt it only fair to warn her it might come to that. It was rather flattering that the other woman had seemed genuinely upset at the idea of losing her.

Anna had rushed over when Sara had explained things on the phone. Sara had been in the middle of packing. Anna had given a shriek of horror when she'd seen Sara screw a silk blouse into the bag.

'Let me do it, I like packing,' she insisted, removing the shirt and shaking out the creases.

'Whatever turns you on.'

'I never thought you'd go back,' Anna mused, rolling up a sweater.

'Neither did I.'

'Well, if he locks you in the cellar or anything, just ring

70

me and Paul and we'll come and break you out. Did I say I'm sorry about Ian?'

'Yes, you did, and it doesn't matter.'

'He's quite nice when he's not drunk.'

'If you say so.'

'Won't you find it difficult living in the same house as the *gorgeous* Sean?' Anna asked, too consumed with curiosity to maintain a tactful silence.

Sara rolled her eyes. One of Sean's visits had coincided with her friend staying one school break and Anna had spent the rest of the next term writing about their fictitious affair in lurid detail in her diary. She read the instalments to her envious school mates on Friday nights.

'He's not gorgeous, he's a despicable rat.'

'You might be right, Sara,' Anna agreed without much conviction. 'But if any man deserves to be called gorgeous, it's Sean.' She gave a wicked chuckle. 'I'll tell you for nothing that if I was spending a night in the same house as him I'd find a reason to wander into his room in something tiny and transparent after lights out.'

The image was one that made Sara feel queasy. 'I feel sure you would.'

Anna was not the least insulted by this acid observation. 'You know, there's something about this thing I don't quite get,' she puzzled.

'That's because you don't have a working knowledge of the way megalomaniacs work. I, on the other hand...'

Sara waved her hand to silence her friend. 'Listen up, if your dad had bribed Sean to marry you, why didn't he just keep his mouth shut when he thought you were lying? And, God, who could blame him?' she added in a disapproving undertone. *'Virgin...!'* she tutted. 'It's a criminal waste.'

Sara frowned. This was one aspect that had bothered her too. 'Does it really matter?'

'You know me, I like things to be neat, and this isn't.

Maybe,' Anna hypothesised, 'he didn't actually intend to make love to you, maybe he just got carried away by his feelings.'

'He doesn't have any feelings,' Sara replied obstinately.

'I've got this theory…'

'Please don't get creative,' Sara pleaded.

'Well, you've always had a bit of a thing about Sean.'

'I have not!' Sara denied hotly.

Anna gave her a look. 'Like I was saying, you've always had a bit of a thing about Sean, but he was this unattainable, glamorous figure clearly out of your league.'

'Thanks!'

'That's the way *you* think. So when the gorgeous guy wants to make love to you, you can't believe your luck, but you *can* believe that he's being paid to do it.'

'So this is about my self-esteem…?'

'It was just a theory,' Anna soothed lightly. 'You haven't told me yet. How was it?'

'Anna!' Sara cried as a hot crimson tide washed over her fair skin. 'I told you we didn't do…*anything*.'

'But you nearly did.'

Sara got even hotter.

'Was it as good as the *big kiss*?' Anna always said *big kiss* in italics.

'Oh, God, I wish I hadn't told you about that!' Sara groaned.

'But you did. So go on, is he as good a kisser as he looks?'

'Yes! Now, if you say another word I will scream.'

Anna made a zipping motion across her lips; her eyes above her temporarily silent mouth were eloquent.

'Where is he?' Sara asked, setting down the holdall Anna had repacked for her—there was enough to last a few days in it, but not enough to give anyone the impression she was back for good.

Charles Leighton, her father's unconventional but highly efficient butler, accepted her presence without comment, even though he'd been present on the last occasion she'd stood in this hall. At that time she'd stated with utter conviction the only way anyone would get her over this particular threshold again was in a body bag!

And here I am, she thought, looking around the beautiful but oppressive entrance... It hadn't changed, and she had no doubt her father wouldn't have either.

'I think he's in the study. Shall I...?'

'I know the way.'

'Of course you do. May I say...?'

A smile glimmered in Sara's eyes. 'Since when was there any way of stopping you?'

'It's good to have you home.'

'It's a purely temporary arrangement.'

'If you say so, miss.'

'Charles! Don't call me *miss*.'

'Just being respectful...'

'Since when? How did you get that shiner?'

He touched the multicoloured area around his swollen left eye. 'A slight altercation down the pub.'

'Those lightning reflexes of yours letting you down?' she teased solemnly. 'Aren't you going to offer to carry my bag up to my room?'

'You've got arms, haven't you, girl?'

Sara smiled, and felt some of the tension leaving her body. 'If you weren't so good-looking I'd hug you.' She hugged him anyway.

Charles shook back his long Rastafarian locks and grinned broadly. 'You, just restrain yourself, girl, I've already got a woman. Now, don't go all soppy on me!' he begged, patting the top of the shiny head pressed lightly against his chest.

Sniffing, Sara straightened up. 'Study?'

'You want me to come?'

'I'd prefer no witnesses,' Sara replied grimly as she squared her slender shoulders.

She lifted her hand to knock on the big panelled door and changed her mind. She took a deep breath before she firmly grasped the handle. When he'd had the particular piece of her mind Sara had every intention of giving him, even *dear* George wouldn't have any illusions over her reasons for being here.

Anxious to establish her inflexible determination from the outset, Sara pushed the door open with so much vigour it hit the panelled wall behind it, causing all the expensive collection of Victorian oils fixed there to quiver.

She stepped boldly across the threshold just as the person slumped in the big leather swivel chair lifted his head from the gleaming mahogany desktop.

The burly figure lifted an arm and dragged it across his tear-stained face. 'Doesn't anyone knock in this place?' he demanded thickly. *'Sara...!'*

Her father didn't cry—he couldn't! But he was! Sara's mind struggled to make sense of this anomaly. Her carefully nurtured antagonism slipped away like fine sand through her fingers. Dread gripped her...not too late, not again...*please*.

George cleared his throat noisily and made a pathetically obvious effort to pull himself together. With a visibly trembling hand he picked up a file from his desk and opened it.

Sara swallowed an emotional lump. Her tyrannical parent looked like a frightened child, which frightened her.

'So, you decided to come back, then,' he grunted.

Sara had never imagined she'd feel nostalgic for her father's dictatorial tone and despotic manner, but listening to his weak, quavering voice she'd have given a lot to see him his autocratic self.

'Are you all right, Dad? Is…?' She was afraid to put her fears into words. 'Has something happened? Hilary…is she…?'

George rubbed the remaining moisture on his lined face with the back of his hand. 'No…no, nothing has changed. She's the same. I just—' His voice cracked.

The totally unexpected scene that met Sean's eyes as he entered the book-lined room slowed his impetuous stride. Just inside the doorway he came to a total standstill. It was with deeply mixed feelings he viewed the tender reunion taking place.

Sara was standing over George's chair, not wielding a large blunt object as he had feared, but an equally devastating tearfully tender smile—at least, it devastated him.

Meanwhile George Stean, the man popularly rumoured in the City to have no heart, had his head turned into her middle and was weeping like a baby, while his daughter stroked his thinning hair. Every so often she bent closer to say something soft and soothing in his ear. The way she was looking at him, the tender, misty light in her eyes could not have been in starker contrast to the spitting hostility she'd shown Sean when they had parted company the previous night.

It was a deeply poignant scene guaranteed to bring a lump to the throat of the most disinterested observer, and Sean was a long way from being disinterested; he was involved in everything to do with the Steans up to his neck.

He was very conscious that one word from him—the same word that would make Sara look at him in a more favourable light—and this touching scene would become a battleground…only a total bastard would say that word now!

At times like a this a man could be excused of wishing he were a total bastard!

He'd had his chance to tell Sara the truth, and pig-headed pride—*how could she think me capable of that?*—had stopped him revealing that it had been George's threat to have her declared an unfit mother that had brought him un-announced to her door... So, it hadn't been what had kept him there, but Sean didn't see there was any point dwelling on this aspect of things or the almost constant ache in his groin.

Mum's best interest came ahead of his libido and it wasn't going to do her much good if George and Sara started bat-tling again under this roof. He'd had his chance and he'd blown it. It felt like longer, but it actually only took him little more than twenty seconds to reach this conclusion.

This decision made, there was no point him being here. This was a private moment and one he shouldn't be intrud-ing on, he *should* leave...the moment of reluctance stretched.

Then she lifted her head and saw him.

Sara gazed in shock into his still, dark features. Her pulses raced; his lean, hard-lined masculine beauty made her throat ache and her heart thud. His lushly fringed eyes were un-fathomable as he gazed back at her, but palpable tension seemed to emanate in waves from his tense body.

She could forgive her father for asking Sean to marry her, but not Sean for going along with the scheme; presumably seduction had been the first step? She couldn't decide what made her angrier: the fact he had started to make love to her, or the fact he hadn't finished what he'd started!

This was slightly contradictory, but nothing much she was feeling made sense.

He hadn't actually lied to her, hadn't said he loved her—*he hadn't needed to*! She'd been a willing and eager partner. She could hardly bear to think of *how* eager.

She lifted a fluttering hand to her throat and saw his burning eyes follow the gesture. At that moment her father cried out and the deepening spell was broken.

Quickly Sara bent forward, colour rushing over her fair skin as she offered what little comfort she could. While she did so she was achingly aware of Sean's silent presence. Though she didn't lift her head or acknowledge his presence in any way again, she knew the exact moment he left.

Inexplicably his departure left her feeling totally bereft.

Despite being prepared, Sara found Hilary's frailness a tremendous shock.

The nurse nodded and left.

'Nice woman, but *so* bossy,' Hilary observed. 'Your dad has just left—he's delighted to have you home,' she revealed happily. 'Did you enjoy your walk?'

Sara forced a smile onto her stiff lips and walked into the sunny room, hoping the older woman hadn't noticed her initial reaction.

'It's a lovely day, and I'd forgotten how peaceful it is here.' The walk in the parkland surrounding the house had been meant to give her time to compose herself and gather her thoughts, unfortunately it had done neither.

She hurried forward and hugged her stepmother warmly. She tried not to notice how she could feel each individual vertebra and rib, even through her clothes.

'Would you be a dear and wheel me over to the window, Sara?' Hilary nodded towards the alcove where a table was prettily set with tea and cakes. 'Don't worry, I'm not incapable of getting around under my own steam just yet, but sometimes when I'm tired...'

Sara nodded and wheeled the chair over to the window indicated. Satisfied Hilary was settled, she sat down herself in the wide window-seat, pulling a cushion onto her lap as she had done often as a child when she'd sat here in the dark watching the badgers outside.

'Is the badgers' set still there?'

Hilary nodded. 'It is indeed.' She smiled with satisfaction as she looked out onto the terrace and the spectacular views beyond; here the land had never been cultivated and the ancient woods came almost right up to the house. 'This is my very favourite spot in the entire house,' she revealed.

Sara looked out blindly over the amazing vista. 'Mine too.' Hilary really is dying, she thought…for the first time it seemed real.

'You don't have to pretend, my dear,' Hilary said softly, catching her hand. 'I know how I look wretched.'

Sara's eyes filled with tears. 'I'm so sorry…I should have been here…' Hand pressed tightly across her mouth, she sniffed loudly. *'Sorry.'* So much for the stoic tower of strength, she thought as she fought to control the sobs that racked her body. 'I'd have come sooner if someone had told me.'

'Sean wanted to tell you. I know he was very opposed to keeping you in the dark. If it hadn't been for George…'

'Sean wanted to tell me? But I thought…he…'

'Yes, dear?'

Sara shook her head. 'Nothing, just crossed wires.'

'Your father generally means things for the best, but I think Sean's right, he is over-protective.'

'Sean said that?'

Her stepmother nodded serenely, quite unaware of how much she'd given Sara to think about.

'Pour us a cup of that nice tea dear Charles has left for us,' she suggested prosaically as her stepdaughter collapsed weakly into the chair opposite her. 'He'll be very cross if we don't drink some.'

'I wish all men were like Charles!' Sara cried, pouring

milk all over the table. If Sean had wanted to tell her, why the hell hadn't he just said so?

'It would make life simpler, wouldn't it?' Hilary agreed, not apparently finding anything strange in Sara's bitter observation. 'Sexy and straightforward.' She seemed not to notice Sara's open-mouthed astonishment. 'I'll be mother, shall I…?' she suggested brightly, taking the china jug from her gobsmacked stepdaughter's lax grasp.

'S…sorry.'

'He is extremely sexy.' Hilary's smile deepened naughtily in a very un-invalid way as the younger woman shot her a startled glance. 'One still notices even when one passes fifty, you know,' she revealed wryly. 'Even when one might be dying. There, it's said, and we need not discuss it again. Now, what has George been recently doing this time to make you so angry?'

Sara, unprepared for this gentle interrogation, blinked. 'He's…' She was trying to come up with a reasonable alternative to *he's been trying to marry me off to your son* when there was a gentle tap on the door and Sean stepped through.

His warm expression took on a forced, stiff quality when he saw Sara.

'Mother…I'm sorry, I didn't know you had company. I'll come back later.'

'Don't be silly, Sean, it's only dear Sara. Join us for a cup of tea. I *insist*,' she added, frowning as her tall son continued to display puzzling signs of reluctance.

'How cosy,' Hilary murmured with a dry sense of humour as she dispensed tea to the silent couple. 'I was just about to ask Sara about her work…' Hilary looked expectantly towards her son. She looked annoyed when he ignored the pointed social cue.

'Sorry,' Sara murmured as her mobile phone began to

ring. As she'd expected, her caller was Rupert from the flat above hers.

'You got my note, then?' She listened while her neighbour assured her there was no problem with feeding the cat and he'd water her plants too if she liked, which made Sara laugh.

'You know that you're a total angel.'

His reply made her laugh again, and blush a lot; Rupert had a *very* earthy sense of humour.

'You have still got your key?' she checked. Rupert had a habit of losing anything that wasn't attached to him. 'You know I packed in a hurry...yes, I know I'm a terrible packer. I could actually do with a few things...' She turned a little away from Sean and Hilary and lowered her voice. 'Toiletries, deodorant and stuff...yes, I probably could do with some more of them too. Top drawer. I'll try and pick them up later. All right...*kisses*.'

'It was Rupert.' As if they really want to know that, Sara.

It was Sean's bored expression that made her perversely expand. 'He lives in the flat above me. He's going to feed my cat...well, it's not strictly *my* cat, more of a stray that deigns to let me feed him.'

'That's nice, dear.'

'Yes, he's going to go in and water my plants too. And pack up a few things I forgot. I'll try and get them later.'

'It's always a good thing to have a neighbour who will kccp an eye on a place when it's empty.'

Sean got up from his chair; it scraped noisily on the wooden floor.

'I've just remembered I've got to go into town...'

He could at least have come up with a more inventive excuse, Sara thought dully as she watched him bend to kiss his mother's cheek.

He looked at Sara. 'I'll pick up your stuff for you if you like.'

'You...?'

'It won't be far out of my way. I'll be back before dinner, Mum. I'll see you then.'

Sara interpreted this to mean that he didn't expect her to be there. He could clearly not bear to be in the same room as her, which made his offer to pick up her things all the more surprising. Unless he'd leapt at the excuse to get out of the room.

After her son had left Hilary looked speculatively at the young woman who was sitting there displaying a great interest in the pattern on her teacup.

'George thinks they're original,' she said, rubbing her own finger over the delicate rim of her own cup, 'but personally I think he was robbed...they're fakes. Not that I'd tell him, of course.'

Sara raised her eyes and smiled. 'Yes,' she said brightly. It was clear to the older woman that her stepdaughter didn't have the faintest idea what she was agreeing to.

'I hope you'll excuse a nosy woman's curiosity, but this Rupert...is he your boyfriend?'

Sara started to laugh. 'Actually, Hilary, I'm not his type.'

'I'm sure you'd be any man's type,' Hilary retorted loyally.

'Rupert's partner is called Derek.'

Hilary joined in the laughter this time.

'You know, I'm so glad you are here, Sara. The boys are such a worry.'

Despite the fact she felt on the brink of total collapse, Sara smiled to hear the two masterful men who didn't have a boyish characteristic between them thus affectionately described. 'They're both tough.'

'That's the trouble, they're bottling up their feelings, putting on a brave front for me, but inside...' She sighed heavily.

Thinking of her father's outburst earlier, Sara remained silent.

'I'm especially concerned about Sean,' Hilary continued. 'You must have noticed how strained he's looking?'

'He does seem to have lost a little weight,' Sara murmured, taking a gulp of her tea. 'But he seems pretty fit,' she added quickly. An image of Sean's greyhound-lean, hardly muscled torso appeared in her head; his bronzed skin was glistening with need. It didn't matter what he'd done, or how shamefully he acted, she still wanted him.

Oh, God!

Fortunately her stepmother seemed oblivious to the hot colour Sara felt flood her neck and face.

'I'm not denying he has a very robust constitution,' she conceded. 'But everyone has their limits.'

Sara, who felt pretty damned close to her own, nodded. Sex and love are two very different things, she told herself... Mind you, put the two together and it must be about as close to heaven as you could get without actually dying.

'Actually, George has come to rely on him pretty heavily. The problem is your father is a bit of a despot.'

A dry laugh was wrenched from Sara's throat. 'No argument from me!'

'And over the years he's surrounded himself with yesmen. Now he needs someone to lift the load from his shoulders there's nobody working there capable of making a decision! You could say he's the architect of his own dilemma. I think this is why he's turned to Sean...' She laughed suddenly. 'Because a yes-man is one thing even Sean's worst enemy couldn't accuse him of being!'

Sara found herself unable to share the joke. 'Well, he certainly said no to me...' The memory of his cold rejection when she'd quite literally begged him to stay brought her out in a cold sweat. 'Enough times over the years,' she added, her eyes sliding away from her stepmother's enquiring gaze.

Her body was still shaken at spasmodic intervals from the devastating wave of sexual longing that had blasted through her when he'd appeared—*and he'd barely even looked at her*!

'In fact a person could be excused for thinking he sometimes goes out of his way to say *no*,' Sara observed grimly.

'He does have very definite views,' Hilary conceded. 'You know, he comes here and sits with me for hours on end and I know he's working late into the night. Then the next day he's at his desk before dawn. I try to get him to relax, but he just smiles and does as he likes. I was hoping that you'd help me...'

'*Me...?*' Sara gasped weakly. Could this conversation get any more uncomfortable? She swiftly learnt it could.

'Why, yes, dear, I was hoping now you're here you could encourage him to take some time off...ask him to take you for a nice dinner somewhere...even the occasional walk. Sean's a great walker. I'm convinced it would do him the world of good.'

'If he doesn't take any notice of you I really don't think he's going to take any notice of me,' Sara choked.

'I think you underrate your influence with him, my dear.'

I'm becoming paranoid, Sara decided ruefully after a suspicious examination of Hilary's face revealed only innocent concern—no sinister hidden meaning.

'I have no influence with Sean.'

'We'll see,' Hilary murmured before, much to Sara's relief, going on to talk about the 'surprise' birthday party her husband was arranging for her.

An hour later it was clear to Sara that her stepmother was exhausted.

'Shall I ring Charles for some more tea?'

'Actually,' Sara began apologetically, 'I'm a bit tired...'

'Of course, my dear, so selfish of me...you go and have a rest before dinner.'

CHAPTER SIX

SEAN hadn't turned up for dinner, which didn't surprise Sara, and Hilary was eating in her room though her father assured her that she usually made the effort. The man himself made no mention of earlier, but he was clearly uncomfortable so Sara refrained from mentioning anything about it either.

Dinner was a strained affair and neither of them said much. Sara refused dessert and excused herself pleading exhaustion, which wasn't far from the truth.

Sara was halfway to her room before she remembered her bag still in her father's study.

'Damn!' she sighed, unwilling to make the half-mile trek to recover it. She'd just have to make do.

She stepped into her old room and almost tripped over the forgotten bag. Alongside it lay another smaller bag; clearly Sean had returned at some point.

'Charles, you angel!' she cried, picking up the larger of the bags and throwing it on her bed.

Everything, she realised, was just the way she'd left it except for one thing...there definitely hadn't been a man on her bed when she'd left...

'What the hell are you doing here?'

Sean dropped the bag he'd caught on the floor and uncoiled his lean length from her bed. The heavy lids lifted from his eyes as they slid over her rigid figure. The action had all the hallmarks of compulsion about it.

'Waiting for you.' And maybe compounding a massive error of judgement...?

85

As if it were the most normal thing in the world for him to be doing!

'And…?' she prompted huskily.

He shrugged 'There's no and. Am I an angel too? I fetched your bag for you.'

'No!'

'That's not very democratic of you,' he complained lightly.

'So sue me,' she growled.

'I met your Rupert.'

'He's not my Rupert.'

He gave a snort of disbelief. 'Well, he must be nearly there. You don't ask total strangers to pack your knickers for you!' He thought of the younger man's blonde pretty-boy good looks and experienced a wave of violent revulsion.

Sara regarded him suspiciously. 'I hope you weren't horrid to him; he's very sensitive.'

What was it with women and wimps? Maybe he ought to try saying he was in touch with his feminine side? 'I was *nice*,' he gritted.

It would be a crime if Sara chose the feeble creep as the man who would introduce her to the joys of sex. Why was it women were suckers for a pretty face? he wondered grimly.

Sara was now deeply suspicious. She resolved to ring Rupert and check he was still in one piece.

'You don't *do* nice.'

'Well, *Rupert* seemed to like me.' The pathetic twit had seemed to be oblivious to the fact he'd wanted to wring his scrawny neck. He had even offered him coffee at his place and had seemed genuinely cut up when he'd refused.

For some reason his reply made Sara giggle.

Sara wiped the grin off her face. 'I'm sure he did,' she responded solemnly. 'Will you stop looking at me like that?'

she snapped, when his searching scrutiny got too intense to bear.

'You're tense,' he observed with a critical frown.

And he couldn't work out the reason for that...?

Sara had actually thought he was blessed with more intuitive powers than that! She closed her eyes for a moment and told herself repeatedly she was cool with finding an incredibly good-looking, virile man in her bed. It was almost incidental that less than twenty-four hours earlier he'd been taking off her clothes and promising to do indecent and deeply delicious things to her.

When she opened her eyes she wasn't cool and nothing that had happened between them felt incidental. Anger flared through her. Hadn't he done enough to mess up her life?

'Don't you think that might have something to do with the fact I walked into my room expecting a bit of peace and privacy and found you? I need sleep, not an argument, Sean. This is a big house,' she continued practically. 'It shouldn't be too hard to avoid one another.'

'I'm not here to argue.'

'Which begs the question...?' Her confident pose deserted her big time when he took an unexpected step towards her. For his one step she took several hurried ones backwards.

Sara exhaled in relief when he stopped beside a small bureau. From under the protective sweep of her lashes—a pretty insubstantial protection—she watched suspiciously as he picked up a bottle and poured some amber liquid into two glasses. They hadn't been there earlier, but then neither had the bottle nor the man, for that matter.

'The good stuff Charles hides from your dad,' he explained, proffering a glass. 'He thought you might need it.'

'He was right,' she breathed feelingly. Not meeting his eyes, she took the glass.

That solves the presence of the bottle and glasses, she thought, but not the man... She somehow doubted he was here to see she swallowed her nightcap like a good girl. Perhaps he'd got wind of Hilary's little idea for her to supervise his 'R and R' and was here to protest the plan.

'I don't burn.' He sounded annoyed.

Evidently the immense efforts she was taking not to touch his fingers had not gone unobserved.

'Yes. Yes, you do,' she mouthed abruptly.

Sean's restless gaze, drawn by the lure of her luscious lips, watched the soft, inviting contours visibly tremble.

'Sara...' he began hoarsely just before she raised the glass to her lips.

He did try to stop her draining the glass, but she twisted away and, batting him off with her free hand, she swallowed the lot. When it was empty she presented him with the glass upside down accompanying the gesture with a triumphal smile.

He folded his arms across his chest and shook his head...as if she'd just done something particularly stupid and juvenile. Because she had done just that, Sara responded aggressively to the silent condemnation.

'What's wrong?' she demanded belligerently. Her actions might not have been the height of sophistication, but damn it she was under stress. She thought she deserved to be cut a bit of slack, not sneered at in that snooty, superior way.

'I suppose you do realise that rum is one hundred per cent proof...?'

Her throat burnt and her head spun a little as the warm glow pooled in her stomach. She felt fine.

'Does that make a difference?'

Sean groaned. 'Charles will have a fit when he hears what you just did. Sacrilege.'

'Savour the nectar,' she giggled with an abominable attempt to mimic Charles's warm Jamaican accent. The giggling part was strange because she wasn't a giggly sort of girl.

'Exactly,' Sean responded drily. Looking at her face, he removed the bottle from her bureau and replaced it in his pocket. 'This wasn't a good idea.' But you had to come didn't you? Suddenly it couldn't wait until morning…

As Charles fell for your casual, 'I'll drop it in, I'm passing her room anyhow,' the voice in Sean's head mocked him.

It didn't seem possible that he'd managed to delude himself this far into believing he had a legitimate reason to be here.

'What are you doing?' she demanded indignantly.

'Saving you a hangover…' He scanned her face, dwelling longest on her pouting lips and overbright eyes. 'Well, maybe not,' he conceded drily.

'It's my hangover, and it's my rum,' she retorted, advancing on him with intent.

Sean didn't try and evade her, and maybe he wouldn't have, but when it actually came to taking positive action Sara was reluctant to frisk him to retrieve her booty.

Indecisively she stood there, her hand extended, her wide eyes fixed on his face her breath coming fast and shallow. This close she could smell the tantalising scent of the expensive cologne he sparingly used and, underneath, the clean, male scent of his body… Her quivering stomach muscles dissolved into a pool of dark, liquid heat.

'You,' she announced huskily as she tucked her hand behind her back, 'are a spoilsport.'

'And you are drunk.' Perhaps this wasn't such a bad thing—at least it put her totally out of bounds.

'On one little sip? *Bah*…' she snorted scornfully.

His eyes narrowed. 'How much have you had to eat today?'

'What's that got to do with it?' Sara swayed belligerently towards him.

Sean placed both hands on her shoulders. 'Quite a lot if it's nothing,' he explained, trying to hang onto his patience. Did the woman not possess *any* normal instincts of self-preservation?

Her lips quivered. 'I don't know why you're acting as if you care!' she flung.

'Maybe because I do.'

Here and now wasn't the place to think about how much. One fact was indisputable: it had definitely been a major error of judgement to put himself in the same room as Sara and a bed... Maybe he should open the door...? And do what, Sean, scream for help?

It was horrifying how much she wanted to believe him. Angrily she pulled away.

'The only thing you care about is money and power! Have you any idea what it feels like to discover you've been bartered like a commodity?' she whispered miserably.

Sean's frustrated breath whistled through his clenched teeth. 'I *have* money and power,' he reminded her.

'Men like you always want more!' she responded dully.

'If that were true why didn't I just keep my mouth shut?'

'That's what Anna said. *She* believes you're misunderstood.'

A perfect stranger was willing to give him the benefit of the doubt but not the woman he loved! How ironic was that?

His sharp inhalation made Sara look up. There was a peculiar unfocused expression in his eyes. He swallowed hard and the look faded.

'And what do you think?'

Sara didn't reply—she didn't need to; her expression said it all.

It was this willingness to believe the very worst of him that goaded him into unwisely adding, 'If I'd wanted to seduce you, Sara, you'd be seduced. I could have, I still could! Maybe I will!' he added recklessly. 'It would make your dad happy.'

Sara's faint hope that she'd been wrong faded. 'There wouldn't be much point once he knows I'm not pregnant.' She'd be telling him the next time she saw him. The only reason she hadn't confronted him earlier was that she hadn't wanted to do anything to spoil the rare rapport between them.

'Maybe I'll just do it for the pleasure, then,' he responded in a goaded manner.

'You admit it, then!' she yelled, throwing her arms wide in an extravagant gesture. 'You came to my place last night with the *specific* intention of seducing me.'

'Just who seduced who?' he blasted back. 'Hell…I didn't mean…' His head fell back and he gazed at the ceiling for inspiration.

Everything he said seemed to be making things worse— so maybe he should just not say anything at all? Maybe he should just quit trying to prove his intentions had been pure and without ulterior motive…well, without ulterior motive anyhow.

'You've forgiven George, couldn't you forgive me?'

'It's not the same thing!' she flared furiously.

'Why not?'

Her eyes slid away from his. '*Dad* needs me right now.'

He dragged a hand though his dark hair. 'Maybe I do too?' Hearing himself say this shocked him almost as much as it seemed to shock her.

Sara lifted her incredulous eyes to his. '*You need me?*'

After a brief struggle Sean managed to stop himself admitting how much…partly because the timing was wrong and partly because he didn't think there was a chance in hell that she'd believe him.

'It seems to me that we all need each other to get through this thing, Sara.'

'Is that what you came here to say?' She gulped. Shame engulfed her. *He was just thinking about his mother and the support network she needed whilst I was thinking about how to crawl between his sheets, which makes me not only totally self-centred but insensitive to boot!*

'There's too much happening right now. This really isn't the right time to work out what's going on between us, Sara.'

Sara caught her lip between her teeth and chewed. 'Is there something going on between us?' She held her breath as his eyes swept over her face.

His big shoulders lifted; his expression remained sober. *'Could be...?'*

Major commitment it was not, but nonetheless Sara did feel a warm glow.

Just when she had decided it was high time she started displaying a bit of maturity, she was crying like a child, not little sobs, but big, gulping, dry sobs that shook her entire body. Big, amazingly strong arms were around her, holding her, comforting her, letting her release her misery on a broad chest.

'I didn't know it would hurt so much!' she kept wailing as she grabbed handfuls of his shirt and rubbed her wet face against his chest.

Sean in his turn grabbed handfuls of bright copper hair and fed it through his fingers, while simultaneously murmuring soothing nothings in her ear. His free hand stroked her slim back from shoulder to buttocks in long, sweeping motions.

Eventually the sobs subsided, until there was just the occasional quivering sigh. Trembling sighs, even deep ones, did not drown out the heavy thud of a male heartbeat. Listening to it, she got a lot less relaxed about the fact she was attached to Sean like a second skin. In fact all the things that had moments before been innocently comforting were now alarming and exciting.

She unpeeled herself from his chest. 'I'm not very good at this.'

'You'll do just fine.'

'Sorry.' She sniffed, patting the noticeably damp patch on his shirt. The dampness made the light fabric transparent…she could see the soft whorls of dark body hair on his chest through it.

'Any time.' He smiled at her and she felt deeply ashamed of her erotic thoughts. Thinking about sex at a time like this seemed desperately inappropriate.

'She really is going to die, isn't she?'

'We really don't know, Sara,' he said sombrely.

'Sean…' Eyes filled with fear lifted once more to his. 'I'm scared.'

'I know.'

Of course he did; Sean knew what she was thinking before she did. She linked her arms around his neck and pressed her body to his. What could hurt if they forgot together for a little while?

'Stay with me,' she pleaded huskily.

I wonder if he knew I was going to do this, because I sure as hell didn't!

There was a short silence. *'No.'*

Sara looked into his hard, unyielding face and gave a hiccough of frustration as he unwrapped her hands from about his neck. Her skin burned with mortification. If only she could go back about sixty seconds…

'You don't like me…you hate me,' she heard herself accuse childishly. She proceeded to make matters worse by adding, 'And don't act as if you don't want me because I know you do!'

Somewhere in the deep recesses of her mind—the part unaffected by this temporary madness—Sara knew she was going to regret her words and actions the next day...possibly sooner...

Sean's eyes lifted from the pouting curves of her mouth; the nerve in his cheek was ticking away like a time bomb. 'What you need is sleep.'

'Don't patronise me, or tell me what I need!'

Anger stirred in Sean's pale eyes. 'I know you've had some shocks and I'm made some allowances...' he began in a low, charged tone.

'I know what I need!' she declared loudly. 'And it isn't sleep.'

And she did—the tangled mess of feeling that had been churning inside her had resolved into a rock-solid certainty. What she wanted was love, not just any old love—she wanted Sean Garvey's love... That being a total non-starter, she'd settle for what she could get.

'What I want is *sex*! Preferably mind-numbing sex!' She stole a discreet look at his mouth from under her lashes; what she saw made her reasonably certain that if anyone could supply this it was Sean Garvey.

'Grow up, Sara!'

His harsh reprimand shocked her into sobriety.

'It hurts. Being grown up hurts,' he explained brutally. 'And you can't get drunk or jump into bed with the first available male every time it hurts.'

'I don't want *any* male. I want you,' she declared angrily. 'And I'm not drunk.'

Too late she realised that this admission had removed the only reasonable excuse she had for talking like this. Now she could no longer claim at a later date that she'd been acting under the influence.

Sean took her chin between his long fingers and looked deep into her eyes. 'And how long will it be before you start wondering if I haven't worked out some secret deal with your father? What did he say when you told him you weren't pregnant?'

'I didn't actually get around to telling him.' She tried to snatch her face away but his grip held her firm.

'Maybe, but he likes the idea of you being someone else's problem. And as we all know I'm some power-mad psycho who's likely to agree to anything.'

'I didn't say that!'

One dark brow rose to a satirical angle as his cynical gaze scanned her flushed face. *'No…?'* he drawled. 'Come off it, Sara, you know this is a bad idea. We've all got to live together under very difficult circumstances—this is a complication we don't need.'

Everything he was saying was true. 'Then why did you come to my bedroom? Wasn't that asking for trouble?' She was damned if she was going to take all the blame.

'Yes, it was.'

'Then why?'

Her words were lost inside his mouth as his lips closed possessively over hers. The driving kiss stole the breath from her lungs and the strength from her limbs. Hand pressed to her lips, she staggered back when he released her seconds later.

'That answer your question?' he asked, pulling open the door.

George was waiting for him.

Sean's hand closed over the door handle. 'This is getting to be repetitive.'

'I've been trying to have a quiet word with you all day.' George Stean considered his silent stepson's stony countenance. 'I'm extremely grateful you got Sara to come home. It went better than I dared hope.'

'I'm happy for you.'

'I knew you'd come through…of course, she's talking

about it being only temporary, but we know different.' He gave a conspiratorial wink.

'I didn't do anything except tell her the truth about Mum. All it would have taken from you was a phone call, George.'

'You're far too modest, my boy.'

The pleased smile that split his cherubic countenance made him look like a jocular Santa. The illusion was spoilt by the ribald chuckle that accompanied his next sly observation.

'Would I be wrong in assuming there are aspects to this little scheme that are not entirely…ahem…disagreeable to you? Not that there's anything wrong with that,' he added, clapping his hand companionably over Sean's shoulder. He encountered a total lack of give in the well-developed steely contour, and his eyes widened. 'I really must start working out,' he murmured, withdrawing his hand. 'Feel free to make use of the gym while you're here. It's very well equipped, or so I'm told,' he added drily. 'Never seem to have the time myself.'

'George, I went to see Sara with the intention…the *sole* intention of warning her about your plans for her baby.'

'You did *what*?' The shrewd eyes narrowed to icy slits as George Stean visibly fought to control his rage. 'But you didn't tell her, did you?' he mused, relaxing.

'No!' Sean confirmed from between gritted teeth.

'Shall I tell you how I know that?' George asked, taking a swaggering step towards the tall, stony-faced figure.

'She didn't spit in your eye when she saw you?'

'You didn't tell her, Sean, because you're not a stupid man. Despite an unfortunate sentimental streak, you have a good business mind. No, you didn't tell her because you know what side your bread's buttered on.'

A quiver of distaste passed over Sean's rigid features as he listened to the jarring confidence in the tycoon's voice.

'The fact is I'm not going to marry Sara for you, not at

any price. There is no subtext here, and before you start I'm not trying to get a better deal. I'm just saying no.'

The cheerful *bonhomie* faded totally from the older man's face as his eyes narrowed dangerously. 'We'll see, shall we...?'

CHAPTER SEVEN

SINCE he'd been staying at Springhurst Sean had got into the habit of having a run before dinner. Used to his own space and his own company, he looked forward to this solitary time. Today he pushed himself harder than usual—he had a lot on his mind.

It was dusk as he approached the front of the house; he immediately spotted the solitary figure standing in the rain. Even at this distance she was radiating anxiety.

The knots in his shoulders it had taken him at least ten miles to lose returned with a vengeance.

'I was waiting for you,' Sara explained as he stopped a few feet away from her. Under the glow of the electric security lights the drops of moisture clinging to his dark hair gleamed. She hadn't expected him to act as if he were falling apart when he saw her, but a little less tranquillity would have been nice. Even at this calamitous moment the sight of him caused her throat to grow dry and her heart to race.

'So I see.'

Hands braced on his hair-roughened, sweat-slick thighs, Sean stood there waiting for his breathing to slow. Her own showed no signs of doing so any time soon.

'I need to talk to you before—' she began urgently.

'Is this about last night?' he cut in tersely.

'Last night?' She shook her head, giving the impression that the events he referred to were already nothing but a vague memory to her, which was pretty much of a kick in the face when you'd spent the entire night and clocked up ten miles thinking of very little else!

'My mistake.'

'You've been gone ages,' she reproached, too distracted to hear the bitter note in his voice.

'And you missed me, I'm touched.'

'This is no time to be clever,' she retorted snappily.

Sean, who had rarely felt less clever, smiled thinly. 'How long have you been waiting?' His restless gaze ranged over her slim, inadequately clad figure.

She shook her head and glanced nervously over her shoulder. 'That doesn't matter. I need to tell you...'

'You can tell me inside—you're getting wet.'

With an impatient frown she dismissed the moisture clinging to her face. 'For goodness' sake,' she groaned in frustration. 'Will you just listen? It's important.'

'If I stand here any longer I'll get cramp,' Sean informed her, catching the heel of his trainer in his hand as he flexed his knee joint. And if he didn't stop staring at her breasts cramp wouldn't be the only thing giving him pain.

'Don't yell!' an increasingly agitated Sara pleaded as she followed him into the hallway. 'They'll hear you.'

'They who?'

'Thought I heard you, man. How was the run?'

'Not too bad.' Sean caught the bottle of chilled water the butler threw at him. 'Thanks,' he added gratefully as he unscrewed the top.

'Your ma was asking after you.'

'I'll look in after I've showered.'

'I got the impression that it was quite urgent...'

Sean stiffened. 'Is she...?'

'She's all right. In fact she looks better than I've seen her in a long time.'

'Then I wonder what the rush is—' Sean began.

Sara stopped tapping her toe and released a noisy hiss of frustration. 'That's what I've been trying to tell you!' she cried, wringing her hands in vexation.

'Then tell away.' With infuriating calm Sean nodded once

more in a matey fashion to a departing Charles before lifting the bottle to his lips.

Watching the rhythmic, muscular movements in his glistening brown throat as the water glugged down made Sara momentarily forget the extreme urgency of her mission.

After wiping the excess moisture from his mouth with the back of his hand and replacing the top on the bottle, he sighed.

It was only when she heard herself produce a weaker, breathier version of her own that she awoke to her weakness and got focused once more.

'That's better. Now I'm all ears...but talk while we're on the move, if you don't mind. The muscles tend to seize up if I stand still,' he explained, rubbing a hand briskly over his muscular thighs before attacking the stairs two at a time.

In theory this sounded practical. In reality keeping up with someone with legs as long as Sean's left her very little breath for anything else. They had reached the door of Hilary's bedroom before she managed to catch his arm.

He lifted one brow to that familiar quizzical angle, the one that always left Sara with the impression he was slightly amused. Well, amused wouldn't last long, not once he knew what awaited him the other side of the door, she reflected grimly.

'Listen, if you go in there before you've listened to me you'll be sorry,' she gritted, hanging onto his arm for dear life. A vindictive person—she ought to work on her vindictive streak—might have let him find out the hard way.

The way she had!

'You're right, we need to talk.' He looked down into her upturned face and Sara knew straight off she'd been wrong about the amusement—there wasn't a trace of humour in his expression. Quite the opposite, he was radiating an explosive tension. It was hard not to be diverted from her purpose in face of that much concentrated emotion.

'No, *I* need to talk, you need to listen,' she insisted doggedly. She grabbed his other arm and tried without much success to shake him.

'It was totally unrealistic of me to expect us to put our feelings on hold.'

'The thing is, Sean...' She stopped, registering what he had just said. '*It was...?*' she began warily.

'Unrealistic and unreasonable. God! We're both living under the same roof.'

'Are you saying one of us should leave?' Hilary's his mother, so I suppose it should be me, she thought.

'No, that's not what I'm saying.'

'I don't suppose you feel like giving me a clue about what you are saying?'

'I can't pretend I'm not pretty uncomfortable about the fact you haven't had any lovers—I mean, it's healthy at your age to experiment, explore your sexuality.' He made it all sound rational and pragmatic but he looked neither. He looked, she decided, distinctly stressed...extraordinary for Sean, who she'd always imagined would look impassive facing a hurricane! 'However, let's not get hung up about it.'

'I'm not hung up about it, you are,' she felt impelled to point out at this juncture. The only person she wanted to experiment with was standing right there looking indecently attractive in skimpy running shorts and a vest.

'I wanted to throttle that gorilla when I saw him with you,' he growled abruptly.

'I actually wouldn't have objected too much if you had.'

'I was jealous as hell.' There, he'd said it. His chest lifted as he drew air into his cramped lungs.

Sara, who had already gathered this, was intensely pleased to hear him confirm it anyway. She suddenly felt incredibly powerful in an irresistible, sexy, man-eater sort of way. Sara had never thought of herself as either sexy or a man-eater. She found it was rather intoxicating.

'God, Sara,' he breathed shakily, stroking the side of her face. The tender action created waves of sensation that started deep in her stomach and worked their way down to her toes. 'I know the circumstances are far from perfect...'

You have no idea how imperfect! Oh, God! As loath as she was to stop him, she knew that she had to tell him what had happened now before she lost the plot completely.

It might already be too late...?

'But I think we'll have to work something out.' His eyes darkened as he gathered her tightly into his arms. This was fine because breathing wasn't a priority with her at that moment. The expression of something more than pain on his taut features shocked her. 'I don't want you to get hung up over some guilt thing.'

'I won't...will you...?'

His lips twisted in a self-derisive smile. 'Probably, but *we have to*!' he groaned, forgetting as passion flared hot and dangerous between them that control was an important factor in any relationship to him.

A current of electricity slammed through Sara as their lips met. She linked her arms about his neck and, sighing deeply, opened her mouth to let his tongue slide deep inside. That was when things really got out of hand!

As their fevered embrace became increasingly frantic Sara was completely consumed by an overpowering need to get as close to him as possible—to achieve this end she squirmed a good deal. She was only dimly conscious that his hands were tugging urgently at the folds of her clothing in order to touch her, lay bare her heated skin.

Her own clumsy exploration was getting more urgent with each passing second. She felt a deep shudder run through his body as her hands slid over his shoulders. When her questing fingers skimmed lightly over his smooth flesh, luxuriating in the tensile strength of the hard slabs of compact muscle just below the sweat-slick surface, he released a ragged groan and lifted his mouth slightly from hers.

'Don't stop!' she whispered.

The blaze of hunger in his eyes stilled her husky protest. Excitement fizzled along her raw nerve endings. Her skin tingled where his fingers lightly touched her as he brushed the stray strands of hair from her hot face. His eyes didn't leave hers for a second as he placed his hand on the back of her neck and lifted the heavy swathe of hair from her neck. Bunching the slippery, flaming silkiness in his fist, he deliberately drew her head backwards.

Sara closed her eyes as she felt his mouth wetly touch the pulse beside the hollow at the base of her throat.

'Do you have *any* idea what you're doing to me?'

'Driving you wild with lust?' she suggested hopefully.

A laugh was torn from Sean's throat. 'You are a witch.'

'And you,' she returned, giving a rapturous little sigh, 'are *absolutely* perfect.' She gave a cry of alarm when, without warning, the door Sean was leaning against opened. Off balance, he staggered sideways with her in his arms to avoid colliding with the figure that emerged

'Oh, there you are, Mr Garvey.' Hilary's nurse, wearing an enormous smile and a uniform that fitted a little too snugly around her ample bosom, held the door open to allow them to pass.

Sean did the gentlemanly thing and waved her through.

'They're waiting for you inside, and may I just say that I think it's lovely?'

Sean, who was using his body to shield Sara's flustered efforts to button up her shirt and make herself look generally a little less ravaged, received this warm observation cautiously.

'Thank you.' He turned to Sara as the older woman

moved away. 'I think…?' he added in a bemused undertone. 'Have you got the *faintest* idea what she's talking about?'

'I'm afraid I have,' Sara admitted. 'That's what I've been trying to tell you…'

'Is that you, Sean…?'

Sean closed his eyes and swore under his breath. 'Yes, Mum.' He mouthed a flatteringly sincere 'sorry' at Sara and went into the bedroom.

With a barely repressed groan Sara followed him inside.

'Open the champagne, George!' Hilary cried excitedly from her propped-up position in bed.

Looking faintly bemused, her son walked towards her open arms.

'I can't tell you how happy I am!' she exclaimed, enfolding her only child in a maternal embrace. 'When George told me I could hardly believe it, could I, darling?'

'No indeed,' her husband agreed. Despite his jovial tone, Sara noticed he was sending some concerned glances in the younger man's direction, and well he might, she reflected grimly. She for one would not lift a finger to stop Sean if he decided to dismember her parent…in fact, she'd help.

More fool me for thinking a few tears meant he was a changed man! she thought.

Her anger was reserved for her father. At some point over the last twenty-four hours she'd accepted that Sean had never had any intention of marrying her—not something that might normally be a cause for celebration, but in this case it removed the last obstacles in her mind. Maybe Anna's theory hadn't been so far off the mark…?

'Come along in, Sara.' Hilary shot the silent figure by the door an affectionate smile. 'You know, I think the girl's in shock. Heavens, I know I am. I won't embarrass you by asking how long this has been going on.'

'Actually, George, it's a bit early for me,' Sean said, looking at the older man, not the glass in his hand. The steady regard made his stepfather look very uneasy, a circumstance that pleased Sara.

'Too early to toast your own wedding? I hardly think so,' his mother reproached.

Sara, her eyes on the unrevealing outline of Sean's broad-backed figure, held her breath, but he didn't fall down or start screaming heated denials. Barely without a pause, he took the glass from her father's hand. Sara, recalling how she'd almost fallen over when it had finally dawned on her that her father had decided to force Sean's hand in this way, was lost in admiration for his control.

'You've got a point,' he agreed smoothly. 'Cheers, every-one.'

Sara, gulping her own champagne, didn't dare meet his eyes. She could only imagine how angry he was feeling and who could blame him? Her father was totally unscrupu-lous…to use his own wife as a lever to force them to do what he wanted. Mind you, he was in for quite a shock when he realised that his efforts to provide her with a husband were unnecessary. Maybe he wouldn't be feeling quite so pleased with himself when he realised there was no baby.

'Now, tell me, when is it to be? Have you set a date? I know some people these days wait until after the baby is born, but…' Sara's gasp was audible. 'I hope you didn't mind, but your father let it slip…quite accidentally.'

Sean shot the older man a look that made him shift un-comfortably. 'An easy thing to do,' he remarked in a voice totally devoid of any discernible emotion.

Sara marvelled once more at his restraint.

'I think it's absolutely marvellous,' Hilary enthused emo-tionally. 'A grandchild.'

'Actually, Mother, there isn't a baby…'

'What do you mean there isn't a baby?' George snapped, glaring from Sara to the tall, imperturbable figure of his stepson. 'Of course there's a baby.'

Sara was quivering with outrage as she spun around to face her father's accusing glare.

'There never was a baby, Dad, except in—' Sean caught her arm and dragged her to his side.

'In our imaginations,' he finished smoothly for her. 'I'm afraid it was a false alarm,' he explained, casting a significant look down into her flushed, stormy features. 'Sometimes when you want something a lot...' He let his words trail off, giving the clever impression that they had been desperate to conceive.

You could do worse than to listen to what he's saying the next time you read something that's not there into his actions, Sara told herself. She knew there was a very real danger of convincing herself her feelings were reciprocated when in reality Sean wanted her body, not a lifetime commitment. She felt a deep pang of envy for the woman who would one day incite these feelings for real in him.

'Of course.' Despite her obvious disappointment, his mother greeted the news philosophically. 'You mustn't get upset, Sara, there's plenty of time for babies.'

'That's what I said, didn't I, darling?' Sean purred, taking her chin in his fingers and smiling tenderly down into her face.

It's not real, Sara, she reminded herself brutally as she started displaying some worrying signs of responding to the tenderness. 'Yes, of course.'

'And in the meantime we've a wedding to arrange.'

Sara viewed the enthusiasm shining in the older woman's eyes with growing dismay. The thought of their impending nuptials seemed to have lent Hilary a new lease of life.

'George, you'll have to make arrangements to fly over the family in New Zealand straight away.' Hilary, a Kiwi by birth, had a lot of family over there.

George looked shocked by this development.

'First class, of course,' Sara added, taking malicious pleasure from her father's startled expression. Though he could be extremely generous like a lot of excessively rich men when it came to spending his money on certain things, he had an irrationally mean streak—with her father it was expensive hotel bills and travelling. He was well known for travelling economy class.

'How many of them?' he asked faintly.

'Why, all of them, of course.' His wife sounded surprised by the question.

'How many were there at last count, Mum?' Sean enquired innocently.

'Without the babies, about forty. It'll be good to see the house filled with young people again.'

'Aunt Gertie is eighty if she's a day,' Sean reminded his mother.

'Is she the one who thinks Dad is a money-grabbing monster who's made his fortune on the backs of the workers?' Sara asked, entering fully into the spirit of things.

'No, that's Aunt Emily,' Sean explained straight-faced. 'Aunt Gertie is the one who thinks he has criminal features—something to do with his sloping forehead, I understand.'

'Don't you think a smaller wedding would be a more sensible option? I'm sure Sara doesn't want a fuss.' George smiled hopefully at his daughter, who didn't trust herself to respond.

This could mess up things between her and Sean completely. Sean was going to be furious and, while she might not be responsible for her father's actions, she might well take some of the flak.

'Having all those people to stay will tire you, Hilary,' her husband insisted.

'George is right, Mum. Why not hire the Grange for the duration instead?' Sean suggested helpfully. 'I hear the new owners spent a small fortune upgrading it.'

'That is reflected in the prices they charge,' George observed grimly.

'George, you wouldn't begrudge spending money on your only daughter's wedding!' his wife reproached.

'Of course I wouldn't…'

Sean set his glass down. 'We're quite prepared to put the whole thing in your hands, George,' he revealed generously. 'Aren't we, sweetheart?'

Sara was flustered by this unexpected appeal for her opinion. In the middle of her panic Sean's eyes meshed with hers. There was warmth in his and part of her desperately craved that warmth, so much so that she briefly lost sight of the fact he was acting a part.

'Absolutely.' She realised it didn't matter much what she said; nobody watching her could have doubted for one second that she wouldn't blindly agree to anything he said. The scary part was that they might be right!

'However, right now, though, I urgently need a shower and someone to scrub my back…?' With a wicked smile he turned towards Sara. 'Any offers?'

Sara was still stuttering her blushing response when he dragged her forcibly out of the door.

When he released her she fell back against the wall and clutched her pounding head.

'I'm so…*so* sorry. I don't know how he could do this…?'

'There are very few things George wouldn't do to get what he wants. You of all people should know that, Sara.'

Sara nodded, feeling her anger surge. 'And very few people he wouldn't hurt,' she added bitterly. 'He's a shark!' she hissed vehemently.

'And you don't expect a shark to have a really good grasp of ethical considerations. As for expecting him to show any—don't hold your breath.'

'Why are you being so philosophical all of a sudden?'

'He really thought he was acting in your best interests.'

'My God, you're not defending him, are you? I hate to be the one to remind you, but we just got engaged.'

'Of course I'm not defending his methods—the guy's unscrupulous. It's just this isn't the right time for a big family feud.'

Sara took a steadying breath. Sean was probably worried she'd let the cat out of the bag in front of Hilary. 'Don't worry, I know that, but, oh, God!' she groaned. 'Why didn't I get round to telling him there was no baby. If I had...'

'There's no point indulging in what ifs, it's a waste of resources.' The total absence of rancour in his voice baffled her.

'I don't know how you can be so calm.'

After a token resistance she let him take her hand and haul her away from the wall. 'This isn't the end of the world.'

'Well, it feels like it!' she retorted. 'I...I'll talk to him.' And say what, she didn't know, but she had to make this right somehow. 'I did try to tell you.'

'I know.'

'But you kissed me and I— '

'Kissed me back.'

Sara's tummy flipped. She decided not to go there.

'What are we going to do?' she wondered anxiously.

'Whatever it takes to make Mum happy.'

Sara looked uncertainly into his stern, uncompromising face, and wondered if that *whatever* included marrying her.

'Of course, it goes without saying that I feel that way too. But...'

'Your support isn't unconditional?'

Sara angled an uncertain look at his face, unable to understand why his dry suggestion made her feel so guilty. 'Well, I won't actually marry you.' Not much, you wouldn't. 'That would be...silly.'

Best not to mention or even think about the mental image

that was even now playing in her head. It was one that she was getting to be pretty familiar with. She was drifting down the aisle towards a tall, incredibly handsome figure to the strains of Mendelssohn. Emotional whispers of 'the perfect couple' and 'I've never seen a groom look so proud' followed her joyous progress.

'*Silly?*' For the first time since he'd received the news of his imminent marriage, his demeanour seemed less than composed.

She gave another nervous laugh as his enigmatic eyes scanned her face. 'All right,' she conceded huskily. 'Criminally insane.'

It seemed essential for both their sakes to lay down a few ground rules. To marry a man who didn't love you, especially when you'd come to the inescapable conclusion you were head over heels in love with him, would be foolhardy and extremely painful.

Fortunately sleeping with him was another matter entirely. This opinion was based on sound logic, and a conviction she might go insane if she didn't! God, how she envied Sean who was only in lust. He would wake up one morning and it would have passed, like a bad head cold... A wave of self-pity washed over her.

Had she been genetically programmed to fall in love with the wrong man? Or was this a purely random twist of fate?

'I don't think it will come to that.'

'But what if—*oh!*' Her eyes filled as his meaning hit her. Hilary wouldn't be with them long enough for it to become a problem. Her fingers tightened around his.

'Don't say that,' she pleaded.

The flicker of raw pain that crossed his face made Sara's throat ache. 'We've got to face facts, Sara,' he told her gently. 'You can't hold out for a miracle.'

'*Why not?*' She closed her eyes and bit her lip. 'Sorry,'

she whispered when she had herself under control again. 'I didn't mean to yell.'

'Don't mention it…been there…done that.' He produced a tissue to dab the moisture clinging to her long eyelashes. His tender actions brought a fresh rush of weak tears to her eyes. She'd cried more in the past twenty-four hours than she had in the previous twenty-four months!

'I've got it,' she mumbled, reaching clumsily to take the tissue from him.

As their fingertips brushed a jolt of neat electricity passed through her. Sara took a shuddering breath, and the jerky movement of her head as she looked up sent strands of copper hair across her face. Her eyes locked with his for a fleeting moment before she looked quickly away. The transient expression she had glimpsed on Sean's face made her wonder if he'd felt something too. Was he remembering the passion that had flared between them on this very spot a little earlier? Up to this point she'd been able to blank out those recollections, but now the door was open she could think of little else!

'I know I'm not being very grown up about this…'

'You've not had long to get used to it.'

'You're being very understanding.'

'Understanding is my middle name.'

'Dying with dignity is not the same as giving up!' she suddenly burst out.

'Oh, Sara!' Sean caught her face between his big hands and tilted it up. 'Don't think that, sweetheart. Never think that, nobody's giving up here or dying, I promise you.' He brushed a few stray strands of hair from her cheek with his thumb. 'Mum's a fighter, I should know. I tried every which way I knew to stop her marrying George.'

'Is that why you glowered all the way through the ceremony?'

'Glowered?' he echoed with mock outrage. 'That was me being a good loser.'

Sara smiled weakly. 'It's good to know even you can't do everything well.' He made no attempt to prevent her drawing away from him. Perversely she immediately wished he had. 'I really got tired of the sound of your name back then. All your accomplishments were paraded before me— Dad had always wanted a son, you see. *Sean* can do this, *Sean* can do that…Sean has a photographic memory, Sean can walk on water. I had these very uncharitable dreams about you falling flat on your face.'

The recollection of other less repeatable nocturnal fancies concerning him made the teasing light fade suddenly from her eyes. She turned abruptly and fingered the gilt frame on the eighteenth-century water colour on the wall.

'I had no idea.' He sounded genuinely appalled by her revelations.

Why would he know? For him she'd hardly existed.

'Don't worry, it didn't cause any lasting psychological damage.' She turned back to him abruptly and shook her head. 'Oh, God, Sean!' she groaned in anguish. 'What a wretched bloody tangle this is. What are we going to do?'

Sean firmly removed the hands she'd clamped over her mouth. 'How about we just go with the flow?'

'Are you mad?' she asked him incredulously.

'Think about it, Sara.'

'That's the problem, I am.'

'Mum will be happy enough organising menus and dresses, all you'll have to do is choose between a cold buffet or a sit-down meal and try clothes on.'

For a wedding that wasn't going to happen!

She took a deep, steadying breath. He didn't know what he was asking her and the only way he'd find out would be if she told him how much she loved him. This wasn't going to happen.

'Sometimes a little lie is justified if it means making someone you love happy. Or are you the truth-above-all type?'

Sara shook her head. Telling Sean she loved him at this point would undoubtedly make a massive impact, but a *happy* Sean…she didn't think so!

'I've no problem with the *lying*,' she admitted frankly. It was better all around if he thought she was a really good actress. 'I suspect it's genetic, I'm actually quite good at it.' She could hardly explain it was him catching onto the fact she *wasn't* acting that had her worried.

Sean looked relieved by her attitude. 'I know it's awkward, but you can play along, can't you?'

'Of course I can.' Any other response would have been terminally selfish.

'Thank you, Sara.' He smiled.

Sara's throat closed over emotionally as her eyes clung to his rivetingly handsome face, refusing all her efforts to dislodge them. She saw the moment the novel idea occurred to him.

'You know, I thought it was just part of the spin when George said Mum had always kind of hoped we'd get together, but maybe he was right.'

It was clear to Sara he thought the idea a real hoot. Sean's expression invited her to share the joke but all she could manage was a weak smile.

'You saw yourself she was delighted and she's certainly never been very keen when I've got anywhere close to popping the question.'

'You've been close?' Sara yelped indignantly. 'Since when?' she demanded.

His amusement she could cope with, it was the speculative light in his silvery eyes that made her rush to fill the startled silence that followed her hot words.

'Do you blame me for being surprised? I thought you made a point of avoiding girls who looked at rings.'

He didn't deny her accusation. 'It's not a conscious thing, I simply don't meet any women with marriage on their minds. They're all too busy with their careers.'

Sara snorted. 'You mean you cross to the other side of the street if you see them coming, more like. Let's face it, Sean, it would take quite a woman to make you abandon your fulfilling role of sex god, especially when you've worked so hard to qualify,' she pointed out sweetly.

'Makes me wonder why you're contemplating becoming another notch in my bedpost...'

Sara gasped. 'I am not...' One dark brow rose to a satirical angle. 'Well, maybe I am,' she admitted. 'But it's not because of your stupid reputation. In fact,' she revealed bluntly, 'it's despite your reputation.'

'What is it because of, then?'

'You're not going to leave this alone, are you?'

'You know me so well.'

'Fine, you want to know?' She waited until he had nodded his dark head before continuing. 'Primarily I'm going to bed with you because I think I might go slightly crazy if I don't... I know that sounds frightfully dramatic, but I'm just telling it how it is.' Her belligerent glare dared him to laugh; he didn't.

'When you're not around I wish you were, and when you are around I wish you weren't.' Her low, driven tone was interspersed by stuttering halts as she drew uneven breaths. 'I can't breathe when I look at you, and it hurts here...' she pressed her fist to her belly '...when I think about touching you...and I do think about it, almost all the time, actually,' she said with a self-derisive grimace. The fire died away from her eyes leaving a soft, wistful expression. 'Does that seem a good enough reason?'

They were several seconds into the electric silence that

followed her outburst before it finally dawned on Sara what she'd said. Her head sank to her chest, she wished like crazy that the floor would open up and swallow her, but she knew it wouldn't. She knew you had to face the consequences of your actions in life.

It went against her nature to apologise for the truth so there was defiant pride in her face when she lifted her head.

'Me, I can't stop thinking about how soft you are.'

Sara released a startled gasp.

'I just want to bury myself in your softness. I've tried cold showers, but I can't be in the same room as you without getting aroused. I've never in my life been so frustrated.'

CHAPTER EIGHT

FOR several seconds they just stared at one another. Sara could feel her nipples thrusting boldly up against the soft cloth of her shirt. Her skin was delicately tinged with an all-over flush of arousal. She was in fact so aroused she thought she might burst into flames any moment.

He might not love her, but being Sean's object of desire might well be better than being the true love of any other man, she thought, moved beyond words by what he'd said.

Or then again she might just be rationalising having an affair with a man who didn't love her. God, but those nuns at her boarding school had a lot to answer for! Not that Anna, who had received the same stern warnings about loose morals, seemed to be similarly handicapped in adult life.

So maybe it's me, she thought.

'Well, it looks like we're not going to have too much trouble behaving as if we can't keep our hands off one another.' She laughed.

After a short pause Sean followed her lead and kept it light.

'And another good thing about this is that George will be so occupied stopping Mum over-exerting herself he won't have time to hassle you.'

'Trust me, he'll find the time. Did you see his face when Hilary said she was going to fly your whole tribe over?' A bubble of laughter escaped her lips. 'It was classic.'

'Well, I thought you entered into the spirit of things rather well. You know, it would almost be worth getting married just to see old George's face.'

'Now that would be going too far…but I might just have sex with you to tick him off.' It was *really* tough to make the laughter sound realistic this time.

While she was speaking Sean's emotions swung violently: they started on deep affront and by the end had swung to violent, uncontrollable lust.

His fierce eyes raked her face. 'You'll have sex with me because you can't not.'

'What are you doing?' Sara gasped breathlessly as he took her hand firmly and proceeded to stride purposefully along the hallway at breakneck speed.

'We are going to my room.'

'Your room?' The fact she was almost running to keep up with him was only partially responsible for her breathless condition. 'What for…?'

He threw her a look over his shoulder. 'What do people usually do in bedrooms, Sara? And don't say sleep.'

'I wasn't going to,' she protested. 'What will people think…?'

'As an engaged couple I hardly think there can be any objections. We have a role to fulfil, Sara. People about to get married spend a great deal of time in bed.'

Sara struggled hard to match his practical approach, which wasn't easy when your knees showed a marked tendency to buckle.

'I thought they spent a great deal of time choosing matching china and cutlery,' she breathed faintly. 'And if you're female it's almost obligatory to starve yourself and go down two dress sizes.' She let out a startled gasp as Sean suddenly swung her around to face him.

'Lose an ounce and I'll be very unhappy.' He growled as, elbows braced on the wall either side of her shoulders, he pressed his body against hers. Sara felt dizzy as the extremity of his rampant desire at present digging into her belly became difficult to ignore. Swallowing, she met his burning eyes.

'Well, as this isn't for real, I won't,' she responded obligingly.

'Some bits are real.' He picked up a strand of copper hair. He let it slide between his fingers; his nostrils flared. 'The way you smell is real—is it you or your perfume?'

'A bit of both, I suppose,' she responded faintly.

'I like it. I also like a lot of other things about you.' His gaze dropped significantly.

'It's been said I'm almost perfect until I open my mouth.' She released a quivering sigh and grabbed his head and squirmed in an encouraging way as he nuzzled her throat.

Sean lifted his head; his colour was heightened. 'What idiot said that?' he demanded.

Looking at the finger, she pointed directly at his chest. 'You—Christmas ninety-nine.'

He grinned. 'Clever girl.'

Sara didn't think it was particularly clever to fall in love with someone who didn't love you back, but she kept this opinion to herself.

'You know that sleeping with someone is the quickest way to ruin a beautiful friendship...'

He grinned wolfishly as she touched the tip of her tongue to the finger he was running along her parted lips. 'How fortunate we've never been friends.'

'Extremely,' she agreed a little wistfully. 'Will you slow down? My legs aren't as long as your—!' she was forced to protest moments later.

Sean solved this problem by sweeping her up into his arms in a masterful fashion.

Sean closed the door to shut out the world, and set her down on his bed.

He didn't comment when Sara slipped fully clothed beneath the duvet, drawing it protectively up to her chin. For several moments she examined the elaborately carved half-tester with an expression of great interest.

'It's very big.' She blushed to the roots of her hair. 'The bed is very big...' My God, did I just say that...? She could hardly bring herself to look at him.

'Extremely big, which is no bad thing for some of the things I have in mind.' Sean couldn't retain his composure in face of the expression of wide-eyed alarm that spread across her burning face. 'You're totally adorable,' he laughed, bending to kiss her.

'Like a clown,' she retorted indignantly.

The smile died from his eyes. 'Like the most desirable woman I've ever met,' he corrected huskily.

'What a nice thing to say,' she exclaimed. 'But don't think you have to,' she added sincerely. 'Say things you don't mean, that is.'

'Oh, but I do have to and I never say anything I don't mean.'

'But...'

Sean laid a silencing finger on her lips to still her protest. 'Don't try and tell me nobody's ever told you you're a knockout.' He took her chin in his hand and turned her face first one way, then the other. *'No way!'* he reiterated thickly.

'They have,' she admitted. 'But they weren't...they weren't...you.'

The kiss was a promise of things to come, the essence of sensuality, yet shatteringly tender. Tears shimmered in Sara's eyes when her heavy lids lifted. A deep sigh shuddered through her as her last doubts dissipated... This might be a reckless, crazy thing to do, but her every instinct told her it was the right thing.

Sean's fingers curled around her jaw before he straightened up. 'Wait for me.'

Sara shook her head. 'I have been waiting for what seems like an awful long time,' she admitted brazenly.

Her husky confession brought a slow, predatory smile of pleasure to his lips. Nervously Sara licked her own lips; they were dry, as was her throat. She could feel her blood pumping, vibrating like a drumbeat through her body. As she watched him he pulled the singlet he wore over his head in one fluid motion. The running shorts followed suit.

He was wearing absolutely nothing underneath.

'Oh, my God!' She stared, not in a covert, tasteful way, but in a mouth-open, drooly way. She couldn't help herself; he was the single most compellingly beautiful thing she'd ever seen in her life! As her covetous eyes slid slowly over him the tight knot in the pit of her belly became a physical pain.

Sean seemed amused by her reaction. He stood there totally at ease with his nudity. In fact he was so relaxed Sara wondered if she might not be a little bit repressed, because she couldn't imagine parading around starkers in front of him that way.

Maybe if it were dark and the lights were off? Whereas Sean was clearly not a lights-out person, which was a pity because the thought of Sean and darkness was a combination that she felt sure had a lot of possibilities.

Sean was watching her reaction with an expression of tolerant amusement. 'You like…?'

Sara gasped and dragged her wayward eyes back up to his laughing eyes. As if he needed any reassurance! She pulled the covers up to her chin before picking a handy pillow and hefting it at him.

He caught it deftly, then tossed it back.

Sara clung to the pillow and her eyes clung helplessly to the tall, laughing figure. Just looking at him made her full heart feel as if it were going to batter its way out of her chest.

'You know damned well I like,' she reproached.

What was not to like? He was absolutely, breathtakingly superb! So superb she could forgive him his complacent smile—actually, on second thoughts, maybe not so complacent…? His expression held a raw, brooding quality that had nothing to do with smugness.

'If you carry on looking at me like that, Sara…' he told her throatily.

'I can't help it.'

Her simple reply made him catch his breath. 'Hold that thought,' he cried, grabbing a towel from the back of the chair. 'Give me two minutes…'

'Don't go!' she yelped in protest, rising to her knees.

'Sara, sweetheart,' Sean pleaded. 'I've just had a ten-mile run. I wouldn't be nice to be close to.'

'I wouldn't mind.'

Sean gulped. He held up the requisite amount of fingers. 'Two minutes,' he promised. 'Unless you want to share…?'

'What? Me…shower? You…?'

'No, you Sara, me Sean. Maybe later, hey?'

Sara slumped back on the bed and groaned with frustration. She listened to the sound of the water running in the adjoining room and wished she'd taken him up on his offer and not acted like some clueless, coy virgin.

Possibly because that's what you are…? Well, not coy, but definitely clueless. In fact, she'd never felt so clueless in her life.

Sean was probably less than the promised two minutes, but it was still long enough for her insecurities to raise their troublesome heads. She kept hearing that husky voice on the phone drawling, 'Hello, darling.' Now, if the voice of experience had a voice, that would be it…no doubt about it.

The duvet lifted and Sean slid in beside her. His hair was

still wet from the shower and he oozed a virile vitality from every pore.

Having a delicious and very aroused naked man stretched out beside her in bed was not an experience Sara was totally at ease with. She found it hard to breathe and when he started kissing her neck and removing her clothes in a slick manner that seemed to indicate he had had plenty of practice—husky voice again—it only reminded her more forcibly of her own inexperience.

He didn't comment on the fact she was lying like a block of wood staring at a distant point on the ceiling overhead, but she felt he must have noticed it.

'I don't think this is working,' she mumbled miserably as she felt him reach for the zip on her skirt. His hand stilled. 'I thought it was a good thing to sleep with a man who knows what he's doing, but maybe I'd be better off starting with someone a little less experienced, at least at first.'

'So I'm to wait around until you *work your way up to me*...?' he enquired in a strained, incredulous voice.

'Maybe we're just not compatible.'

'Is that a fact?'

She was miserable, tears were seeping from beneath her closed eyelids and sliding down her cheeks, yet he didn't even sound put out. After all the anticipation it was a dreadful anticlimax...and she'd been hoping for the exact opposite, although being a realistic girl and knowing things didn't happen the way they did in romance novels she'd accepted that certain things took some working at. She'd have settled for getting halfway there—it would have been a lot farther than she'd ever got before!

She felt the bed springs creak and heard a good deal of rustling. It seemed safe to assume that Sean was calling it quits. And who could blame him? Somehow she couldn't picture the owner of the sexy voice on the phone going all cold and aloof.

'To make an informed choice I think you need to give this a bit longer than thirty seconds.'

Sara opened her eyes and discovered Sean had emerged at the foot of the bed, the duvet was around his waist and his dark hair was attractively ruffled. He must have burrowed his way there...the image of him under the covers made her tummy muscles quiver violently.

'I mean, for instance, is this unpleasant?' He drew her foot towards him and ran a finger over the arch.

A tiny tingle shot up her leg.

He waited, his expression expectant.

'No...'

'On a scale of one to ten?'

'Don't be silly.'

'Seven and a half being better than all right. Two being don't go there.'

She shot him a resentful look; only someone extremely insensitive could think there was anything funny about discovering you were as good as frigid.

'And this...?' His thumbs began to massage the soft pads on the ball of her narrow foot. The slow, circuitous motion had a strangely enervating effect.

'Mmm...' Sara felt some of the tension trickle from her tight shoulders.

She gasped and her eyes snapped open when she felt the warm wetness of his tongue run over the sole of her foot. 'That's...that's...' her bottom lifted off the mattress as he licked and nipped his way to her ankle... 'extraordinary.'

'Good, we'll start from there.'

And he did; he worked his way extremely slowly all the way up her legs, tasting and touching, or so it seemed to Sara, every centimetre of flesh. By the time he had reached the soft, highly sensitised area on her inner thighs she was sobbing with pleasure.

'Don't stop!' she pleaded.

'The last thing on my mind, angel, I promise,' he responded throatily.

She sensed him settle between her parted thighs.

He stayed there motionless for several moments, contemplating with burning eyes the shallow, rapid rise and fall of her breasts, before exhaling gustily.

'Watch me,' he suggested softly.

Sara's heavy lids lifted in time to see him tuck her knees up beside his waist—her legs, in fact her entire body, felt like hot wax that he could mould into any shape he desired.

'I respond well to suggestions,' he elaborated, pushing up her skirt to expose the soft curve of her lower belly and the tiny pants that didn't quite conceal the soft fuzz of red curls between her legs.

The shocking idea of tutoring a man in what she enjoyed was a new one on Sara. *Suggestions…!* At that moment she'd have been hard pressed to give her full name.

He slanted a hooded look towards her. 'Feel free to come in at any point.'

Sarah felt as if she were living some erotic dream as she watched this beautiful, rampantly aroused man bend over to press his parted lips to her soft stomach. Liquid heat pooled in her lower abdomen as all her muscles tensed.

Her body jolted when she felt his fingers slide under the lacy edge of her pants. Her excitement mounted dramatically as he began to stroke and caress his way in a tantalising advance-retreat style towards the aching, moist centre of her body.

'I want to taste you, been thinking about it for ever…'

Sara moaned and slid her damp palms over his shoulders.

'Really…?' He seemed not to register the weals her nails raised on the surface of his smooth skin.

'Really.'

'Then do it—!'

Her ribcage expanded and she gasped sharply at the first

shocking contact of his tongue. She moaned softly as he continued to taste and tease while his hands anchored her restless body to the bed.

'Oh, my…?'

He lifted his dark head. 'You like that?' His voice was thick and slightly slurred.

Sara half lifted her head from the pillow. The unfocused theme extended to his eyes, where pale irises were almost swallowed up by his dilated pupils. She couldn't prevent her glance from straying to the firm outline of his strong, sensual mouth…heat washed over her body as she thought about the exquisite pleasure those skilful lips could administer.

'Eight and a half!' she lied before collapsing back. Lying, long legs splayed in an attitude of abandoned bliss, she waited for him to continue driving her sweetly out of her mind.

This time when he removed her skirt she was highly co-operative. Her pants followed, then he slipped the buttons on her shirt and his fingers pushed back the thin fabric of her bra until her taut, aching breasts were exposed.

'Sweet heaven…!'

There was an electric silence as his hot, hungry gaze roamed over her body. It seemed to Sara that under Sean's tan his naturally olive-toned skin was strangely pale; maybe this pallor had something to do with the tension that was emanating from him in almost visible waves. Breathing almost as hard as he was, Sara raised a hand to touch his flank; she felt a quiver run through his body.

Silently she reached up for him, a sensual smile of invitation curving her soft lips. Still he didn't touch her.

'Oh, God, Sara, I want you so badly!' he groaned.

The needy, raw note in his shaking voice amazed and excited her. 'How much more encouragement do you need,

Sean?' she asked, grabbing hold of his shoulders and pulling him down to her.

She felt laughter rumble in his chest as his mouth closed hungrily on hers. Sara slid her fingers into his thick hair and kissed him back, moaning as his tongue stabbed deep into her mouth and then meeting it with her own.

While he carried on kissing her his big, clever hands moved over her body divesting her of the remnants of her clothing, moulding her aching breasts, teasing her burning nipples until her entire body was on fire for him.

When he sensed her hesitation he rolled onto his back and, taking her hand, laid it firmly against his body. That was where his desire for control ended; he seemed more than content to lie there and watch her make her own discoveries.

'How about we go for a ten?'

'Isn't that a bit ambitious for the first time out?'

'Trust me, apparently I'm a sex god.'

'In that case I'm all yours!'

Sean resisted the base urge to slam into her and looked for any sign of hesitation on her face—though God knew what he'd do if she changed her mind now. He could detect none. Her fingers meshed in his hair as, every individual muscle and tendon stretched to breaking-point, he carefully lowered himself over her. He knew he would never forget the soft sound of her amazed gasp or the expression of wonder that spread over her damp, flushed face as he slid slowly into her.

Sara was too occupied assimilating the incredible sensation of being filled by him to register his total stillness for some few moments.

'Is something wrong?'

'Not a thing.'

Her eyes slid to the point where their bodies were joined

and a fresh wave of heat washed over her. 'You have no idea how glad I am this is you.'

'I'm pretty glad about that myself.'

Sara, totally absorbed by the strange and indescribably wonderful sensations as he moved slowly within her, barely registered his hoarse response.

CHAPTER NINE

'WELL what's the verdict?' Sean asked some time later.

Sara rolled over onto her stomach and propped her chin up on her hands. Legs crossed at the ankles, her toes waved gently back and fro as she pushed the silken fall of rich red hair from her eyes. Taking her time, she examined the bare-chested figure lying beside her. It felt gloriously decadent and indulgent just to look at him… It's allowed, the happy voice in her head sang. You can look and touch any time you feel like.

For now.

Sara frowned. This wasn't the moment for realism; this was a moment for optimism and bathing in the glorious rosy afterglow of Sean's love-making. Her eyes darkened dramatically as she relived the stupendous moment the shattering climax had shaken her body.

'It wasn't half bad,' she conceded huskily.

'And the other half?'

She ran a finger over one pebble-hard male nipple and smiled when he swallowed. 'Oh, that was sheer, unadulterated bliss.'

'It gets better.'

Sara felt sceptical, but she was prepared to indulge him—actually she was prepared to do just about anything he asked. Maybe she'd mention that a little later. The thought of what he might do with this information sent a shivery little shudder up her spine.

'Oh, there are infinite ways to make love, we've barely even scratched the surface.'

'With so much to cover ought we to be lying here doing nothing?'

The way she smiled at him made nonsense of his theory about getting in control of his mental faculties once they'd made love. One sultry look and he was a lost man.

'Always supposing you're up to it?' Her back arched like a cat as his hand swept down to her spine before settling on the firm curve of her bottom.

In response to the taunt Sean lunged for her. She made a token show of laughing resistance as he hauled her on top of him, token because in actual fact there was no place she'd have preferred to go. The tussle and his casual display of superior masculinity had a very stimulating effect on her libido, which was odd because Sara had never found muscles a turn on before—maybe it just depended on who they were attached to...?

'At your age you should pace yourself...umphh!' The air escaped her lungs in one gasp as he sealed their bodies at hip level. The erotic pressure left no doubt whatsoever as to his powers of recovery!

'My God, I can't get enough of you!' he groaned, covering one pink, tight nipple with his mouth.

Sara moaned. 'But I think you should make the effort!' she gasped earnestly.

Sean was still laughing when the door unexpectedly swung open. With a startled cry Sara instinctively ducked under the sheets. She had a fleeting image of her red-faced father marching into the room before she pulled the duvet over her head.

'Just what the hell are you doing?'

Sean, quite relaxed about the disturbance, rolled onto his back and tucked one arm behind his head. 'Pretty much what it looks like,' he confirmed mildly.

An inarticulate sound of fury emerged from the older

man's throat as his face got several shades darker. 'You come into my house, sleep with my daughter!'

'You're such a hypocrite!' Sara cried, emerging in a tousled state from the tangle of blankets.

'Hush, Sara,' Sean soothed. His face hardened as he turned back to the older man. 'She's got a point, George, it was your idea.'

George Stean gave the younger man a look of loathing and turned to his daughter. 'Is it true? Are you really not pregnant?'

Sara considered the question in light of recent events. 'It's too soon to tell,' she replied honestly.

She felt Sean stiffen beside her and turned towards him. 'But it's not likely.'

Her comforting response didn't seem to have the desired effect on Sean, who now for the first time looked pretty shaken. If he looked like this now, she thought, imagine what his response would be if I told him in a few weeks' time that we had got unlucky... Clearly the idea of her being pregnant scared the hell out of him. Not an unreasonable response, she told herself, trying to stifle the first stirrings of unease.

'And this is your idea of revenge, I suppose.'

Something inside Sara froze as she listened to her father's accusation. She waited tensely for Sean to throw scorn on it.

'No, this is my idea of pleasure,' he corrected. 'But you're right, George, I don't like being manipulated,' he admitted grimly.

Any reminder to the effect that he had not actually been a willing co-conspirator, or for that matter a co-conspirator at all, would clearly be useless while George was feeling he'd been made to look a fool. This wasn't about his daughter's moral welfare. As far as the tycoon was concerned Sean had beat him at his own game—he was the sort of man who thought of things in terms of winning and losing and he'd never got the hang of being a gracious loser.

'It wouldn't surprise me if you knew she wasn't pregnant all along…you kept quiet to see what you could get out of it. You've abused my trust,' George announced dramatically.

'What trust? You don't trust anyone and never have.'

From where Sara was sitting that didn't seem such a bad attitude to adopt. She'd jumped in with both feet. The fact she hadn't even considered unplanned pregnancies proved this.

'Oh, I suppose this is all spontaneous! Do me a favour!' George snorted.

Spontaneous enough to induce him to have unprotected sex for the first time in his life! Who was he kidding? That wasn't even an excuse, let alone a good one! Not for what he'd done… His expression grew grim as he contemplated his criminal carelessness.

He glanced towards Sara and discovered she was looking at him; for the first time he noticed the dark shadows beneath her grave eyes as if she hadn't had a good night's sleep in ages. Sleeplessness was a permanent state of affairs for new parents… Hell, she was so young, and he was a selfish bastard. He looked away as he felt the oppressive weight of guilt land directly on his shoulders.

'Huh, when you found out she wasn't pregnant you knew you wouldn't be able to get your hands on the company so you thought you'd sleep your way into the family and my money,' George accused wildly. 'I'd let the company go to the wall before I'd let you take control now, Garvey.'

'The talk in the City is it's halfway there.'

Sara saw her father's colour deepen alarmingly. 'And I don't need two guesses who started those rumours.'

'Grow up, George. It's your obsessive need to control people that has placed us in this ridiculous situation. We'll just have to make the best of it. Mum's happy, so you have achieved something.'

George looked slightly mollified by this reminder. 'She is, isn't she?' His volatile temper appeared to have run out of steam. 'I suppose I'll just have to fly those damned relations of yours out,' he grumbled. 'But you keep that psycho auntie of yours out of my way.'

'Which one?' Sean asked.

Sara looked from one man to the other in total bewilderment, unable to get her head around the abrupt cessation of hostilities. One minute they'd been acting as though they hated one another, the next they were calmly discussing wedding arrangements!

'All of them.'

'Done. Why the sudden hurry?'

'There's no hurry, but Hilary has the bit between her teeth now and there's no stopping her. A woman possessed,' he reflected with an indulgent smile. 'I haven't seen her look this positive for a long time. I think it's about having something to look forward to, but don't worry,' he added swiftly. 'I've thought of a way around it that will keep Hilary happy and you a happy bachelor. Someone I know can arrange for an actor to play the vicar—that way everybody's happy.'

'I'm speechless with admiration,' Sean assured his stepfather drily. 'I'm curious, is there a lot of work out there for fake vicars?'

'Actually,' George admitted, 'he's usually a stripogram vicar, but I believe he's very convincing. Well, I'll leave you to it, so to speak...' He grunted nodding casually to his daughter.

When he left Sara flung herself face down and moaned. 'That's all I need—a vicar ripping off his pants while I'm saying "I do"...!'

'How do they rip them off, exactly?' Sean asked curiously.

'Velcro.' It was easy to see the idea of marriage was something of a joke to Sean.

'I bow to your superior knowledge. I suppose you've got to see the funny side to it,' Sean appealed, his attention fatally distracted by the sight of her bottom swaying gently.

'What funny side?' she asked grimly as she hauled herself into an upright position. 'Why do I get the feeling I'm almost an incidental extra?'

'You tell me,' Sean responded unhelpfully. 'That was your dad being your dad. Why do you let him get to you?'

'*He's* not the one getting to me.'

Sean regarded the narrow back she presented him—surely this was symbolic?—with narrowed eyes. '*Meaning...?*' He laid a hand on her shoulder. 'Talk to me, Sara.'

Talk? She couldn't help herself. Her uneasy suspicions were getting uneasier by the second. '*Meaning*, why am I here in your bed?'

'If you don't know I must have been doing something wrong.'

'I *thought* I did.'

'I'm sensing you already have a theory,' he replied at his driest and most daunting.

'*Is* it possible you're...*making the best of a bad situation*?'

Sean closed his eyes, partly to shut out the suspicious hostility in hers. Now that would teach him to watch his mouth.

'Or is it worse than that? Did you really do this just to get back at Dad?'

Anger prevented him from saying the words that would soothe the situation; it stopped him reaching for her.

'You've caught me out.' Sean held out his hands palm

up. 'Fair cop, I'll come quietly,' he promised. 'George has hardly been off my mind all night…it was quite a turn-on.'

Sara blushed fierily. 'There's no need to be sarcastic! You came back here the other night after…'

'You kicked me out.' He was dimly aware in some objective portion of his brain that anger was totally out of proportion with what was happening. Was it too much to ask that she trust him?

Sara was beginning to feel sick. This was hardly the first time they'd rowed, but it was definitely the most potentially damaging. What she'd actually wanted was him to laugh away her concerns and tease her about her insecurities, but this was getting serious.

'You must have had the opportunity to tell him I wasn't pregnant.'

'As did you.'

'That was different.'

'I thought it might be. Let me get this straight—am I on trial here?'

She opened her mouth to deny this cold question and out popped a tight-lipped, 'I don't think it's unreasonable, given the circumstances.'

'Given your total lack of trust.'

Swinging his long legs over the edge of the bed, he stalked over to the wardrobe and pulled out a short robe. It was black and reached mid-calf; when he belted it around his waist it fell open, exposing his bronzed, perfectly developed chest to Sara's helplessly interested gaze. He looked sinfully sexy and about as approachable as an iceberg.

Sara felt a surge of resentment. *He* was acting like the injured party, that was rich! She was the one who had had to sit there while they'd talked about her as though she hadn't been there. Hadn't she read somewhere anger was a common response when a guilty party was challenged…?

'Are you denying you're wondering about my motives?'

She recognised straight away that the fact he was clothed—*just*—and vertical immediately, whether by accident or design, gave him an unfair advantage in an argument.

'Well, you didn't come looking for me until my dad waved the company under your nose, did you?' Please laugh, say it's rubbish, hug me, for God's sake, the voice in her head screamed.

He showed no signs of doing any of the above.

'You really do have a self-esteem problem, don't you, Sara?' he observed, unwittingly echoing Anna. 'Do you actually believe that the only reason a man would want to sleep with you is for financial gain? Or is it just—' he derisively drew inverted commas in the air '—*men like me*? You know, I'm heartily sick of being continually tarred with the same brush as your dad whenever it suits you.'

'Attacking me is a pretty good way of avoiding the question,' she observed dully.

'You want to know why I didn't come calling—fine! I didn't want to be attracted to you. I was fighting it, in denial even. I thought sleeping with you would come with too high a price tag…and, my God, was I right!' he drawled. 'This is exactly the sort of thing I wanted to avoid.'

'The truth, you mean.'

'God, you're totally paranoid,' he gritted furiously. 'I don't know what benefits you think I'd get from sleeping with you.'

As he was regarding her with palpable distaste it didn't seem likely intense pleasure was the answer he was hinting at. His attitude struck her as totally unjust; she'd displayed a perfectly understandable unease and he'd accused her of being paranoid! She wanted a few soothing words and she'd got a lecture!

'If sleeping with you was the way to get my greedy mitts on the damned company, why did I wait? It was perfectly obvious ever since I kissed you in my office it wouldn't take a lot of effort on my part to get you into bed.'

Sara gave an outraged gasp. 'I believe the popular term is ''gagging for it''!' she gritted, bouncing up and down in the bed with sheer agitation. 'My God, you really do think a lot of yourself, Sean.'

'As far as Stean Holdings goes, your father needs me a hell of a lot more than I need him. He was losing his edge even before Mum got ill, but that was the clincher. He doesn't want to admit it to himself yet, but he needs help.'

Sara didn't want to find his tone of conviction pretty compelling, but it was hard not to. If he hadn't got on his high horse all this could have been put right without anybody saying anything they might regret. Not that Sean looked as if he was regretting anything; he was clearly in his element destroying her. Well, just as well she found out at this stage that he was just as much of a control freak as her father.

'I might be forced to give George a hand some time soon, but it's not something I'm crazy about, more a family obligation. I promised Mum.'

'Did you promise her you'd sleep with me too?'

'As we're getting married I think she just took it for granted we would be.'

'Not unlike you.'

'It wasn't exactly an unreasonable assumption to make under the circumstances.'

'Well, I wouldn't take it for granted I'm about to hang around here for you to insult me!' Wrapping herself in the top sheet, Sara slid gracefully from the bed...at least, that was the theory. In actuality her foot got tangled in the voluminous drape and she almost lost her balance.

Sean's hand shot out to steady her, a reflex action because she imagined he'd be delighted to see her fall on her face.

'Thank you,' she said icily.

Sean elaborately removed his hand from her elbow. 'I take it this is goodnight.'

'If circumstances didn't make it impossible it would be goodbye!' *Stop me.*

He didn't; he just stood there looking stupidly noble and frighteningly sexy with his arms folded across his chest—the stiff-necked pig!

The sight of him made her forget her resolution not to mention his other *woman*. She knew she was on shaky ground as they'd never discussed exclusivity. She'd thought about confronting him...issuing an ultimatum: If I'm not enough for you forget it, or, I'm not interested in being part of a harem, but the awful truth was she hadn't been totally convinced he'd have given the answer she wanted to hear.

If that had happened, she hadn't wanted to risk putting her own resolve to the test. What if she hadn't had the guts to walk away? The idea haunted her—she'd never considered herself a weak person, but with Sean she was different.

'Not missing a phone, are you, Sean?'

'As a matter of fact...' His eyes narrowed. 'Did I leave it at your flat?'

'Yes, you did. One of your girlfriends called, she didn't leave a name but she seemed pretty sure you'd know who she was. It's nothing to me if you have kinky conversations with your bed-mate of the moment, but it's a bit much when you act as if you're as innocent as driven snow...'

'*Kinky* conversations...?' Sean's face bore a fascinated expression as he scrutinised her starkly pale face.

'Well, I only just stopped her giving me a run-down on what she was, or should I say *wasn't*, wearing!' Sara choked. 'Maybe you don't call that kinky...'

'God, wait until I tell Penny...' he said when he'd stopped laughing in a nasty, grim way.

Sara's expression of scornful contempt turned to horror.

'You're going to tell this woman about me in bed!' She gulped.

Suddenly Sean didn't feel like laughing. Not only did his Sara think he was a lying, conniving cheat, she thought he was an insatiable stud too! In the midst of his anger it struck him like a ton of bricks. *My* Sara. Oh, God, it didn't seem to matter what she did, or what outrageous thing she said, he couldn't let go.

'Well, actually, I was hoping to post the intimate details on the internet before I turn in, while things are still fresh in my mind. That way I can share the lurid details with a wider audience.'

His sly, sardonic tone made Sara's cheeks burn with mortification.

'Don't worry, Sara, what has passed between us will remain private. No doubt in time we'll be able to forget it ever happened.'

'Of all the horrible things you've said to me, that is the meanest!' she exclaimed without thinking.

Her impassioned declarations clearly puzzled him. 'What do you mean?'

'How would I know what I mean?' she half sobbed. 'I don't analyse what I'm about to say, I just say it!'

His brows lifted as he surveyed her tear-stained face. 'It *shows*. However, I've never heard anyone defend their right to talk gibberish with more conviction,' he conceded drily. 'Tell me, did you go through my pockets at the same time you swiped my phone?'

'I did not swipe your phone, you left it behind!'

'You had no immediate intention of returning it, then?'

'It wouldn't be any use, I drowned it!' Not in any mood to explain her cryptic explanation, she almost ran from the room.

Charles, who was walking in the opposite direction as she

was returning to her bedroom still draped in her sheet, didn't bat an eyelid as she swept majestically by.

'Goodnight, Sara.'

'Goodnight, Charles.'

Sara, who slept very little, came down to breakfast late. She had worked out her survival strategy for the duration of her stay. Top of the list was never being alone with Sean, next came avoiding all unnecessary physical contact, including kissing, and behaving in a calm and rational manner at all times—no more jealous tantrums!

In the kitchen Charles and his beautiful girlfriend Angeline, who shared his flat over the stable block, were seated at the big table. So was Sean. *Damn!* She'd forgotten that, like her, he preferred to take his breakfast in here rather than the more formal setting of the dining room.

She could hardly turn around and run so, chin held at a determinedly jaunty angle, Sara walked forward, nothing in her manner betraying the fact her heart was trying to pound its way out of her chest and she half expected her weak knees to give way at any moment.

'Is there any coffee going?' she asked, dividing her smile democratically between everyone—ignoring Sean completely would be as much cause for comment as her screaming insults or ripping off his clothes.

It was actually quite hard to sound spontaneous and casual when you were proceeding with the stealth of a bomb-disposal expert. One false move, one careless word and the bomb would explode...or maybe she would and all the truth would just spill out of her!

Just thinking about *that* made her blood freeze!

Charles surveyed her rigid face and fixed smile. 'You've heard, then,' he said, getting to his feet.

'Heard what?'

'Ah...my mistake,' Charles murmured under his breath

as he glanced quickly across to Sean. There was an expectant pause, as if he was waiting for the other man to speak up. When he didn't respond Charles grabbed a coffee-pot off the stove. 'Sure thing, Sara, there's always coffee.'

Sara frowned. She was getting the distinct impression that she'd walked into the middle of something. You didn't need to be psychic to sense the almost palpable buzz of expectancy in the air. A sick feeling of dread knotted her stomach as she hurried forward; her immediate thought was that something had happened to Hilary. The defensive disdain slipped from her face as anxiety pushed her personal concerns to one side.

'What's happened? What should I have heard...?' When her wide-spaced eyes automatically sought out Sean there was no remnant of her carefully managed neutrality in the vivid aquamarine depths; the last thing she was worried about just now was the sort of image she was presenting. 'Will someone say something?'

Sean pushed aside his half-empty coffee-cup and ran a hand through his dark hair. It was a weary gesture and if the tousled condition of his normally sleek raven thatch was any indicator it wasn't the first time he'd used it this morning. The air of tightly controlled tension about him was more pronounced as she got nearer, as was the heavy shadow along his jaw...he hadn't shaved. The dark shadow emphasised the photogenic angles and hollows of his heartbreakingly attractive face.

'They called about two hours ago.' He inhaled deeply. 'They've finally found a match.'

'Match...?'

'For Mum. As none of us was suitable, a bone-marrow donor from Los Angeles has been matched to her.'

'Oh, Sean, that's marvellous!' Sara gasped, her face alight with delight. 'It is, *isn't it*...?' she appealed uncertainly.

'It's promising.'

Sara frowned, not understanding his restraint.

Charles stepped forward and filled Sean's cup. 'Enough caffeine to keep you going for a week,' he promised. He glanced towards Sara. 'They'll have to see if she's fit enough for the treatment first—isn't that right, Sean?'

Sean nodded, grateful for the prompt; he was having a hard time concentrating. 'Yes, and even if she is fit enough, and there is a definite *if*, the chemo will effectively knock out her own immune system and make her vulnerable to any infection. A head cold could kill her,' he explained with a calm, clinical objectivity that was deeply at odds with his body language. 'Then there's the possibility of the transplant not taking. A lot could go wrong.'

Sara's heart ached for him, it ached for them all, all the people who would be a lot poorer without Hilary in their lives. She could see why Sean wasn't permitting himself optimism—he just couldn't stand the idea of having that confidence crushed.

'But there's hope…?'

Sean's eyes blazed as he got to his feet. 'God, yes, there's hope, Sara.' His edgy smile faded just before he opened his arms wide.

Without a second thought Sara walked into them.

Sean rested his chin on top of her glossy head and breathed in her sweet smell as she wrapped her slender arms around him. By the time she pulled back the overpowering fatigue that had gripped him had passed and he could actually string a thought or two together.

She looked at him worriedly. 'You've got to be positive,' she told him forcefully.

Sean looked down into her fierce face with an expression that eluded her. His lopsided smile appeared as he saluted smartly. 'Yes, ma'am!'

Sara was relived that he looked a little more normal…a little more Sean. 'So what happens now?'

'George and Mum are at the hospital at the moment. The consultant is running some tests. Apparently we'll have the verdict this evening.'

'Are you going to the hospital?'

'I thought I would a little later.'

'Well, don't go without me, and shave before you go—your mum will hate the designer stubble!' she announced positively.

Sean lifted a hand to his chin. 'Under the circumstances I hardly think she'll notice.'

'She's your mother, mothers notice such things—it's in the job description,' she told him firmly. 'You arrive looking like that and she'll assume you're not taking care of yourself properly,' she added, clinching the argument.

While Sara shared that worry for Sean's health, she parted company with his mother on the subject of his unshaven appearance. Rather disturbingly she found the air of dangerous dissipation it gave him extremely attractive. She was gripped by a compelling desire to run her finger over his cheek...

'Any more orders?' Sean asked, looking more amused than annoyed.

'*Suggestions.*'

He bowed his head. 'Of course.'

'I was wondering if Hilary needed anything?'

'I hardly think so. The room she's in at the clinic is more plush than most five-star hotels I've stayed in.'

'That means it's totally impersonal.'

'Point taken,' Sean conceded.

'How about some of those little truffles you do, Charles...?' Angeline suggested. 'Hilary can't get enough of them,' she reminded her multi-talented lover.

'Well, I suppose I might persuade Cook to let me use the facilities under the circumstances.'

'Brilliant idea, and perhaps some photos.' Sara knew her

favourites were on the piano in the sitting room. 'I'll just put some things together...' She drained a coffee-cup, not her own but nobody seemed to notice, and headed purposefully towards the door. 'When are we leaving...?'

'Slow down! Take a breath.'

'But...'

'I know you want to feel as if you're doing something, we all do, but there's no point making a frantic dash to the hospital only to sit there twiddling our fingers all day.'

Sara's face fell as she recognised the truth in what he said. 'I'd prefer to sit there than here.'

'Trust me...sorry, I forgot, you can't do *that* can you?' Could you sound any more bitter and twisted...? He regretted his self-indulgent, spiteful snipe even more as he watched all expression bleed from her animated face, leaving it stiff and wooden. 'How about a compromise—just give me time to take a shower and make myself a bit more presentable, and there's a bit of business I need to attend to—it won't take long—and we'll head off?'

'Whatever you say.' Last time he'd offered to share the shower. 'I'm sorry if I was pushy—I suppose I just wanted to be...be part of it.'

'You are part of it,' Sean protested.

Sara shook her head. 'Hilary's been ill for months and I didn't know. This morning nobody woke me to tell me what was happening. I'm sure you all had better things to do. I just wish...'

Sean frowned. 'It all happened so quickly this morning, we just thought you might as well sleep. Nobody was trying to exclude you, Sara.'

'No, just protecting me, but sometimes, Sean, that amounts to the same thing.'

CHAPTER TEN

HILARY was delighted with the things Sara had selected to bring. She got her husband to place them to her satisfaction around the hospital room.

'Now, that looks so much cosier,' she said, picking up the silver-framed picture beside her bed of the chubby-faced baby. 'This is my favourite,' she confessed. 'You were a beautiful baby,' she told her son.

And an even more beautiful man, Sara thought, casting a covetous glance in the direction of the tall, loose-limbed figure beside her.

'Please, Mother, you'll make me blush.'

'And why not...? Some of the things I've read about you in the newspapers over the years have made me blush, but that's all over now, isn't it?' she added with a complacent smile in Sara's direction.

It seemed to Sara there was a lot of talk of blushing but she was the only one actually doing any!

George completed his game of solitaire and looked up. 'Anybody for poker?' he asked.

'George, dear, you cheat.'

'Everyone cheats in poker,' her husband defended.

'The sad thing is he actually believes that.' Hilary sighed, regarding her husband with rueful affection. 'Maybe I'll play later, dear, but just now I have something to ask these two young people.' She extended her hands towards Sara and Sean.

Apprehensively Sara laid her hand in Hilary's very thin one and stood there expectantly while she sensed Sean doing the same.

'I shouldn't be asking you this,' Hilary admitted with a self-conscious grimace.

'Don't be silly!' Sara exclaimed, her smooth forehead pleating into a frown of denial. '*Anything* we can do…isn't that right…?' She looked across to Sean to support her.

He slowly nodded, aware his fractional hesitation had probably earned him Sara's contempt.

It was classic Sara, jumping in with both feet before she knew what she was committing herself, and in this case him, to. Sean's exasperation was coloured by tolerant affection because he knew her impetuous responses were inspired by her genuinely warm and generous nature.

His own commitment was a lot less a leap in the dark than Sara's because he was pretty sure he knew what his mother was about to ask.

'Now, I know you were both looking forward to a big wedding with all the trimmings.'

'Looking forward might be a *bit* of an overstatement, Mum.'

In other words he'd prefer to have his appendix out with no anaesthetic than marry me, thought an ultra-sensitive Sara, choosing to put a rather extreme interpretation on his light words.

Hilary, taking the words in the spirit they were intended, shook her head and laughed. 'Men! You act as if the wedding day is not important to you, but I for one don't believe it.' The teasing light died from her tired eyes. 'Seriously, it is my dearest wish to see you get married, but if I go ahead with this treatment the fact is I might not be around to see it…'

'Hilary!' her husband cried in protest. 'That's a ridiculous thing to say—you're going to be fine.'

The desperation in her father's eyes brought the sting of tears to Sara's. In her heart his devotion to Hilary made her able to tolerate—*sometimes*—his other faults.

'Yes, George, I really do hope so, but you're the one who always says only a fool ignores the odds. I'm not being morbid when I say this, but there is a good chance that I'll never live to see your wedding, which is why I was hoping...' She took a deep breath and looked from her son to Sara while drawing their hands together. 'That you'd be willing to marry here tomorrow...? I know it's an awful lot to ask at such short notice.'

'I'm all for intimate ceremonies. So long as the most important people are there, the where and how don't much matter to me.'

This sincerely voiced sentiment brought a lump to Sara's throat.

Tearily Hilary smiled up at her son and mouthed *thank you*.

It gradually filtered into Sara's shell-shocked brain that all eyes were fixed expectantly on her! They thought she was Sean's important person! Gulping, she fixed a suitably light-hearted smile on her stiff lips.

'Looking like a meringue just isn't me.' She felt Sean's fingers tighten fractionally on hers.

Hilary lifted her own hand from the entwined fingers of the young couple and gave a deep sigh. 'I can't tell you both how grateful I am,' she breathed. 'My birthday and your wedding on the same day. My, you'll be in double the trouble if you forget that date, Sean!' She laughed.

'I hardly think that's likely,' Sean responded, his eyes on Sara.

'Of course, if they don't give me the go-ahead on the treatment the same urgency won't exist...we could wait and go along with the original idea.'

Unspoken in the room was the knowledge that this wait couldn't be too long either.

'Actually, Mum, I think I'd prefer it this way, just the

people that count...' One corner of Sean's mobile mouth lifted in an ironic smile. 'And George, of course.'

This made everyone laugh, including her father; the laughter, Sara decided as she wiped the tears from her cheeks, had acted as a release valve for all the intense emotions seething in the room.

Sara thought Hilary, who had settled back on the pillows, looked exhausted; evidently Sean was thinking the same thing.

'You look tired, Mum.'

'Well, actually,' she admitted with a yawn, 'I am rather. Do you all mind if I take a little nap?'

They all immediately assured her they wouldn't.

'I think I'll just sit in the chair and snooze a bit myself,' her husband decided.

'Why don't you take Sara for a nice lunch, Sean? The results won't be back until around four,' his mother urged.

'Hungry, Sara?'

'I wouldn't mind some fresh air.'

'You should eat, my dear,' Hilary said worriedly.

Sean dropped a kiss on her brow. 'Don't worry, Mum, we're living on love.'

Sarah doubted he knew how much his flippant words hurt her.

'Not in public, *please*,' George groaned theatrically from behind the financial pages. '"The world loves a lover" is one of the most inaccurate statements ever,' he grumbled. 'Unless you are in the first flushes of romance, the sight of people with their tongues down one another's throats does nothing but incite jealousy and nausea in your average man in the street, and in my opinion should be made an offence.'

'Really, George,' his wife laughed. 'You are the most unromantic man.'

'Thank you, dear,' her imperturbable spouse responded.

'Do we have your permission to hold hands?' Sean asked mildly.

'Holding hands is where it all starts,' George observed darkly. 'Though I know you've got past that stage.'

Sean's grin widened as Sara blushed deeply. 'Right, I'll switch my phone on in case we're needed—oh.' He turned back. 'Did I give you my new number?'

'Yes,' Hilary confirmed. 'What happened to your old one?'

Sean stood to one side to let Sara go through the door. 'Sara drowned it,' he explained.

'Why,' Sara demanded angrily, 'did you say that?'

'She asked and what can I say? I cannot tell a lie.'

'Since when…?'

'You did well in there,' he acknowledged unexpectedly as Sara selected the stairs in preference to the lift.

'Still got a thing about enclosed spaces?'

Sara nodded.

'I did think you were going to faint at one point.'

'Are you surprised? A bit of a bolt out of the blue hardly covers it.' It was hard to tell from his expression what Sean thought about finding himself forced to go through with a fake wedding ceremony. He could hardly be happy about the prospect, but he appeared to be coping with the situation a lot better than she was.

'Not really.'

'You mean you were expecting it?' she yelped.

'Hardly that, but if you were actually planning to get married and there was a chance your mother wouldn't be around to see it, wouldn't you bring the date forward?'

'But we weren't actually planning to get married. I know…' She raised her hand to forestall his inevitable response. 'Hilary doesn't know that. I just don't see how we can pull it off at such short notice,' she fretted, running the tips of her neatly trimmed nails back and forth across her teeth. 'What if this stripogram vicar isn't available? Have you thought of that?' She glared up at him, close to outright panic.

There were so many things to go wrong...and in her experience when things could go wrong they inevitably did.

'No, I can't say I had.'

'And what about afterwards? If Hilary recovers, how's she going to feel when she learns the truth? It seems to me you haven't thought very far ahead at all.'

'*If...?* What happened to a positive attitude, Sara?' His dark, well-delineated brows drew together in a forbidding straight line. 'As for looking very far ahead,' he continued grimly. 'No, I haven't done that.' His bleak eyes lifted from hers as he transferred his gaze to the floor. 'In fact, I'm trying very hard not to think more than an hour or so ahead.'

Sara's hand came up to cover her mouth. Horror at what she'd said flowed over her. So much for being supportive! She gazed miserably at the unrevealing sweep of dark lashes lying across his cheeks before her head dropped in shame.

'Oh, God, Sean, I didn't mean it like that,' she whispered. '*Please* believe me...I just open my mouth and all this stupid rubbish pours out...' she told him urgently.

'I do believe you.'

Sara breathed a sigh of relief. 'Thanks. I don't know, but maybe you'd like some time alone? We could meet up back here later if you like,' she offered.

'And I thought you were here to offer a bit of moral support?'

'I am!' She caught the tail-end of his sardonic smile as she lifted her head. The blood flowed into her pale cheeks. 'I was trying to be considerate,' she gritted.

'Clearly it's a strain.'

Their eyes met and the hostility faded from hers. Her wide mouth drooped at the corners as a wave of despondency washed over her. 'You have no idea,' she grunted, looking away.

'Because of my lack of finer feelings, no doubt?'

Because you're not in love and I am, she felt like yelling back, but now wasn't the time or place for such revelations. 'Listen, if you want company, fine, but I'm not actually hungry. I need to get some fresh air, not to sit in some posh, overpriced restaurant.'

He shrugged. 'Strike posh, overpriced restaurants. How about we pick up some sandwiches and go to the park to feed the ducks? '

'The park...?' She'd expected him to leap at the opportunity to get rid of her.

'Unless you have a problem with ducks too?'

'No, of course not.'

Listening to him, Sara couldn't help but contrast his flexibility and forbearance with her own surly display of irritability—she didn't emerge from the comparison well. She took a deep breath. About time you made an effort, my girl!

'In fact I *like* ducks.'

'Just not me.'

Sara's head tilted back. Sean wasn't looking at her—in fact, he appeared to be looking anywhere *but* at her.

'Is this where I'm supposed to reveal I find you totally irresistible?' As if he didn't already know.

She expected Sean to come back with some appropriately acid quip, but he didn't. In fact he didn't say anything at all for several moments.

'It would have been nice.' He gazed with brooding intensity down into her upturned features. 'But it had to be spontaneous, the moment has passed.' He turned abruptly from her and led the way down the steep flight of steps.

A gulf bigger than the widening physical one seemed to grow as the uncomfortable silence stretched.

'Sean, I think we should talk about what has happened.'

He turned his head and paused momentarily, his hand on the curved banister.

'Why?'

Sara reached a new level of exasperation. 'How can you say that?' she reproached. 'Are you trying to tell me it won't bother you even a little bit to stand up before people who know us and mouth words you don't mean? It's a mockery! The wedding ceremony is…is *sacred*,' she cried in a throbbing undertone.

His lips curled. 'It's so sacred, in fact, that some people do it more than once,' he sneered, venting his scorn.

His cynicism didn't surprise her. 'So you'd condemn the entire institution because some people don't get it right first time. That seems a bit harsh.'

'I'm not condemning the institution. It just seems to me that some people think that marriage is the big day…the wedding cake, the nervous best man, the drunk bridesmaid. Whereas in reality marriage is the next forty years, but only if you work damned hard.'

Sara's eyes widened in surprise. 'For a man who's never getting married, you seem to have given the subject a lot of thought.'

'Who said I'd never get married?'

'Why, nobody, I just assumed.' She coloured. 'You mean you would get married. *For real*?' A deeply depressing picture of herself as a guest at his glitzy marriage flashed before her eyes.

An expression she couldn't quite pin down slid across his dark, autocratic features. 'I try not to deal in absolutes.'

Sara tried but she just couldn't let this claim pass unchallenged. 'You were pretty *absolute* about me being a depraved nymphomaniac not so long back.'

His unwavering glance didn't drop, but she had the satisfaction of seeing a trace of discomfort in the clear depths of his extraordinarily penetrating eyes.

'I've come to expect a certain degree of, erm…*eccentric* behaviour on my part where you're involved.'

With a puzzled frown Sara tried to make sense of this confusing observation.

'Let's just say that it's not inconceivable that I may marry. When I do, I'm going to make damned sure it's only the once.'

Sara wondered if there was any significance in that *when*. Not if, when! A man who actually had someone in mind might say when. The question turned her thoughts in the direction of the sexy voice on the phone; it was a direction she didn't much feel like going. She never had liked the name Penny.

'Me too…not that I expect to…'

She suddenly sank down onto a step. Bringing her knees up to her chin, she buried her face in her hands. 'I hate myself!' she wailed.

For a moment Sean looked down at the dejected figure at his feet, struggling with an almost overwhelming impulse to crush her in his arms.

'Move over.' Sniffing, Sara wriggled her bottom up several inches to accommodate Sean, who sat down beside her.

'We're blocking the stairs,' she observed with an extra loud sniff. 'I think that's probably against fire regulations.' She stretched out one foot in front of her and wiggled it gently in the air. 'If fire broke out now it's highly likely we'd be termed a fire hazard in the accident report.'

'Now there's a nice cheery thought. The fact is,' he announced with brutal candour, 'you've always been a hazard, Sara.' Mainly to my sanity, he thought as she raised hurt puppy-dog eyes to him. 'So no change there. Now, when you've finished changing the subject, do you think you might get around to explaining just why you hate yourself?'

'Because I'm terminally selfish and shallow. I should be thinking about Hilary.'

'You are; we all are.'

Sara pursed her lips in full self-flagellation mode. 'But I'm also bothered about *me*…how all this is going to affect *me*. How will I cope with tomorrow, how *I* feel about being partnered off with you. Hilary's life is balanced on a knife-edge and I'm…'

Sean stretched his legs out so that her thigh was jammed tightly against his. She was overpoweringly conscious of the heat and strength.

'You're what, Sara?'

'I'm wondering if you like my hair like this.' She picked up the fat plait from her shoulder and flung it back with a grimace of disgust. 'Wondering if you're going to kiss me. Oh, God, I can't believe I just said that!'

Wiping the moisture from her cheeks, Sara lifted her head and discovered Sean was watching her with an expression that made her pulse leap.

'How would you feel if I did kiss you?' he rasped, taking her chin between his fingers and leaning close. Close enough for her to feel his breath on her cheek and see the tiny jagged nick where he'd cut himself shaving that morning. This was the only mark on an otherwise even-toned skin.

'Are we talking hypothetical kisses here?'

'I'm not real good with that abstract, conceptual stuff,' Sean admitted throatily.

The way he was looking at her mouth made the pit of Sara's stomach dip dramatically.

'In that case I can't say for sure, but I think it's a safe bet that part of it would involve me behaving in a manner likely to cause public offence—or at least my father. So maybe we shouldn't do this.'

To her utter and total dismay he straightened up and nodded his agreement. 'You're probably right.'

Sara watched in disbelief as he vaulted energetically to

his feet. She didn't care how disappointed he sounded, she wasn't going to forgive him in a hurry for applying the brakes so brutally.

He held out a hand for her, which she ignored. 'Don't sulk, Sara.'

'I'm not!'

'I don't trust myself to stop.'

Hot excitement slid through her body at the forceful explanation. *'Oh!'* As responses went this one seemed woefully inadequate, considering.

The hand was once more extended and this time Sara took it. His fingers stayed curled warmly over hers as she came to her feet.

'I don't suppose it's an entirely appropriate time.'

'The time's fine, it's the location that leaves something to be desired.' As if to support this opinion the echo of a door somewhere above them being opened echoed down the stairwell. 'And don't start thinking Mum would have any problem with this, she'd be the first person to tell us to take everything we can from every second of the day…you don't get them back.'

Whilst this simplistic philosophy naturally appealed to her, Sara could see some serious flaws in it.

'Sometimes taking what you want has consequences.' Could falling in love be classified as a consequence?

'Don't worry, I won't be careless again.'

Sara flushed. 'I wasn't thinking about *that*.'

'Well, I am,' he replied grimly. 'Come on, let's go and feed some ducks.'

Sara consulted her watch. 'That must be a record,' she mused as Sean hailed a taxi to take them back to the clinic.

'What record would that be?' Sean asked.

'We've spent three hours twenty-four minutes together and we haven't had a row.'

Sean gave directions to the driver and slid in after her. 'What about Tom Jones?'

'That wasn't a row, it was heated discussion.'

'My mistake,' he said, looking amused.

'And I've decided to make your appalling taste in music exempt for future research purposes. It would just wreck my pie chart. You don't think I know what one is, do you? But actually I—'

'Thank you, Sara.'

Her startled eyes were drawn to his; they were warm, almost tender. 'Thank me for what?'

'Thank you for trying your best to take my mind off...things.'

'I don't think I did that well,' she replied, thinking of the number of times she'd caught him consulting his watch.

'Perhaps I should have tried the other method of distraction.'

'You should have said.' Sara smiled. 'What was it?'

He caught her hand and, turning it palm up, ran his finger along her life line. 'You have a long life ahead of you.'

Long and lonely...? Sara's throat ached. 'You were going to tell my fortune?' She dabbed the beads of sweat that had broken out over her upper lip; his touch was sending ripples of shivery sensation around her entire body.

'No, I thought of booking us into a hotel room for the afternoon.'

His rich voice flowed over her like thick molasses. When his eyes, hot like molten metal, claimed her own she was almost zapped into next year by the blast of sharp sexual longing that hit her.

'I suppose you're shocked and disgusted?'

Sara licked her lips and shook her head. Her heart was thudding; she was shaking like a leaf from head to toe. 'Try so excited I can hardly breathe.'

Something primitive flared in Sean's eyes. Hungrily he

scanned her aroused face, dwelling longest on her lush lips and glazed eyes; far from not breathing, she seemed to be breathing very hard indeed. He swallowed.

'*Now* she tells me!'

'You didn't ask.'

'And if I had?'

'Do you really think if I had to chose between spending an afternoon in bed with you or with ducks I'd choose ducks?' she exclaimed, releasing a long, tremulous sigh.

His lips quivered. 'Thank you…*I think*.'

'We're here, mate,' the driver called back cheerfully.

Sean gritted his teeth and swore under his breath. 'I could get him to drive once around the block…?'

Sara was sorely tempted. 'We shouldn't.'

'You're right, of course. Still, we have tonight—don't we?'

Mutely Sara nodded. She might not have much when they went their separate ways, but she was determined to take some perfect memories away with her.

'It's tradition. I don't want you two seeing each other in the morning. In fact,' Hilary mused, 'it would be best all around if you stay at your own place tonight,' she told her son.

'Oh, no!' Sara wailed. 'That is… I mean…' With three people waiting expectantly for her to continue, she dried up.

Sean put down his glass—they'd just finished toasting the news that Hilary had been judged fit enough for a bone-marrow transplant—and put his arm across Sara's shoulders. Gratefully she leaned into his body.

'I think Sara is trying to say my moving out seems a bit unnecessary. Is that right?'

Sara nodded. Good, Sean would think of something. She had complete faith in his ability to think on his feet.

'But Mum's right, Sara. I think we should do things right.' He patted her arm in an insultingly avuncular fashion.

'You do…?' This was her red-hot lover…?

'Start as we mean to go on.' More patting.

Sara gave him a deeply disillusioned glare and eased away from him.

'Excellent!' Hilary approved.

CHAPTER ELEVEN

SARA had retired to her room straight after dinner. Now she actually had the time to read the latest thriller by one of her favourite writers she found herself unable to progress beyond the first page.

With a discontented sigh she returned the paperback to the bedside table, and looked aimlessly around the room. She pulled her foot onto her lap and regarded her bare toenails speculatively—perhaps she should paint them...? Sean would probably approve; it was *traditional* for a bride to spend the time leading up to her wedding pampering and polishing every inch of her body into movie-star glossiness.

It was way too late for her to reach those rarefied heights, but she could at least smooth off a few rough edges. A trawl through her make-up bag revealed an unopened pot of polish. Tongue caught between her teeth, Sara began to apply a coat of glossy polish to each nail. The frown line of concentration between her feathery brows deepened as she contemplated Sean's sudden approval of things traditional.

There, all done. She surveyed the finished effect. *Not bad.* She lay back to wait for the polish to dry.

Her severe expression softened slightly as her restless gaze came to rest on the outfit neatly hanging on the hook behind her door.

It had taken her half an hour to select the ensemble for the next day. She had decided in the end that her cream silk shift was the most bridal-looking thing she had, and after further deliberation she had added a pretty antique beaded stole. She took longer picking out suitable undergarments...though if tonight was any indicator her efforts might be wasted, she thought, looking at the gossamer scraps.

They were the sort of items meant to inspire a desire to rip them off, which was probably why they'd lain untouched at the bottom of her drawer since she'd bought them at a saucy lingerie party! After the party she'd been disgusted with herself for giving into peer pressure at her age.

She still couldn't believe that Sean had accepted their separation so meekly. She understood he didn't want to upset Hilary, but to not put up any sort of argument...! Clearly it was no big deal to him... Her brow puckered; he'd acted as if it was a big deal in the taxi. She had been seeing his face through a haze of lustful heat at the time, but she didn't think she could have got it *that* wrong... She reviewed the image stored in her memory, and her stomach dipped sharply. No, he'd *definitely* wanted her!

Maybe he'd remembered he had a previous engagement...?

'You can have him!' she yelled, picking up a one-eared teddy and chucking it at the door.

With the sort of timing that would have taken a film crew half a day's rehearsal and several takes to achieve, her bedroom door opened and the tall figure that stepped inside caught the airborne bear a split second before it hit him in the face.

He closed the door. 'Cute outfit.' He seemed to be showing an unhealthy interest in the lingerie component!

Sara hitched her cotton nightshirt up over her shoulder so it promptly fell off the other. 'How did you get in?'

Sean patted the one-eared teddy companionably on the back and placed him a rocking-chair. 'Charles let me in the back door.' His eyes slid to the smooth bare shoulder. 'I considered climbing the drainpipe, it had dramatic impact in its favour, but the very real possibility I'd fall to my death swung it in the end.'

'You wimp!' she told the man whose idea of fun was dangling on a rope over a chasm or pulling himself up sheer cliff faces by his fingernails.

'I could go back outside and climb in if you prefer, although you're going to feel pretty responsible if I break something vital.'

His attractive whimsy brought an edgy smile to her lips. 'I still can't believe you're here.'

'Where else would I be?'

'At your flat.' She winced to hear the petulant note enter her voice. 'It's *tradition*.'

'I was at my place, and I will be again before anyone's awake.'

'In other words you lied.'

'I didn't think you had a problem with that. You must admit, this way everyone's happy.'

'*Everyone…?* That's a pretty big assumption.'

'So you're not happy to see me?'

Happy didn't really do justice to the breathless relief she'd felt when he'd walked into the room. 'This is typical of the sneaky way you operate. You could at least have told me what you were up to,' she added crankily.

'*Are you happy to see me?*' he persisted.

Her eyes skittered nervously away from his.

'I like the toes. What colour do you call that?'

Sara looked down and began to pull the wads of cotton wool separating her toes. She pressed her lips together. 'Perfect pearl,' she muttered.

'No, that's your skin. It has a translucent lustre that is truly incredible…' He released a stark, sibilant hiss.

Sara tried frantically to ignore the trickles of heat sliding up her spine. 'How many times have you used that line?' she croaked.

He didn't reply, just carried on looking at her with bone-melting intensity.

'You know, it would do you the world of good if some-one were to take you down a peg or two, Sean Garvey. You're way too smug and full of yourself.'

'You think so…?' The notion seemed to afford him some wry amusement. 'Are you planning on being that person?'

She caught her full lower lip between her teeth and gave a short laugh. 'That's not likely, is it?'

'How so?'

'Where I'm concerned your confidence is fully justified, Sean.' Maybe she'd feel better getting it out into the open? Or then again maybe she'd feel like a total idiot! 'Where you're concerned I'm spineless and totally hooked. I've just joined the ranks of your brainless bimbos, which must be music to your ears.'

'It's a damned concerto, but not for the reasons you think. You don't qualify as brainless or bimbo.'

'Is this a blonde thing?' she wondered dully. Penny would be blonde.

Grinning, he shook his head. 'I was glad to hear you say that, because I'd started to wonder if maybe I'd read it wrong and your sweet offer this afternoon actually had more to do with pity than lust.'

She gazed at him in blank astonishment. 'Are you mad?'

'That possibility is never very far from my mind at the moment.'

'I wouldn't sleep with anyone out of pity, I'm not some…some…tart with a heart!'

His warm laughter rang out. 'I did play the compassion card pretty heavily, and you may be older but basically you are the same kid who sold her precious CD collection to send a donation to that famine appeal.'

'God, you remember that! The *last* thing you inspire in me is pity.' The longing on her face was unconcealed as she gazed at him.

Sean's slow smile was one hundred per cent danger.

'Sara,' he rasped. 'Those undies…did you by any chance buy them for me to take off?'

'No, I bought them to be one of the girls,' she admitted. 'But you can take them off, only not tonight. I'm saving them for tomorrow. Tonight,' she explained huskily, 'there won't be anything for you to take off.'

A marvellous sense of recklessness gripped her as she took hold of the hem of her nightshirt and pulled it over her head in one smooth motion.

A stark silence followed her actions.

His silvery eyes slid over her body before locking with hers. She shook back her hair and it fell thick and soft down her narrow back.

He wanted to bury his face in it; he wanted to bury himself in her.

'*Oh, my God!*'

Her embattled brain couldn't figure out how she came to be lying, her hands pinioned either side of her head, with Sean's heavy body pressing her down into the mattress.

She considered her position. 'This is good,' she concluded thickly.

'It's about to get better.'

It did.

When Sara woke the next morning Sean was gone. She might even have thought that the night before had been an erotic fantasy, if her aching body hadn't supplied ample proof of their nocturnal activities.

After her shower she pulled on a robe and went down to the kitchen for coffee. Charles was placing trays of canapés in the fridge.

'This wasn't a good time for Cook to come down with the flu,' he observed, looking more harassed than she'd ever seen him.

'I don't expect he did it on purpose,' Sara mused, inspecting the tray in his hands. 'They look good, but the kitchen doesn't,' she added, looking around the big room— every inch of work surface was covered with dirty crockery and open packets. Charles seemed to have used every utensil there was.

'Well, don't look at me! I'm only prepared to take this multi-tasking stuff so far and I'm already way past that point! I like to cook, but catering is much too stressful for my taste,' he revealed, closing the big fridge with a relieved sigh.

'I think you're brilliant.'

'Yeah,' Charles agreed with a complacent grin. 'So do I. You,' he added tetchily, 'should have stayed in your room. I was going to fetch you up a tray—*eventually*. It's traditional.'

'I'm not a very traditional girl.' She wished she had stayed in her room though; the cooking smells were beginning to make her feel nauseous.

'Sleep well?'

Sara pursed her lips and refused to rise to the very obvious bait. 'Yes, thank you, Charles.'

'I'll have to sit down for a minute first,' George informed his daughter when they reached the top of the stairs. 'Why you won't go in lifts, I don't know,' he gasped as he struggled to get his breath.

'That's because you have a very bad memory. I got stuck in that lift when I was five.' She'd been separated from both her parents on a holiday, nobody in the lift had spoken English and she'd been totally hysterical by the time they'd been rescued...some forty minutes later. 'Anyhow,' she added, directing her gaze towards his generous middle, 'it wouldn't do you any harm to take the stairs once in a while.'

'Thank you for that. Now, if you're quite finished making personal comments...' With a grunt he heaved himself up out of the chair. He held out his arm. 'Ready…?' George looked down into his daughter's pale face; the image seemed to shake him.

Sara nodded.

'You know, you look lovely; just like your mother.'

Sara's face flushed with pleasure. 'Do I really?'

She looked down at the simple cream shift dress she wore and then at her indistinct reflection in the tinted plate-glass panel that sectioned a small sitting area from the main corridor. She saw the image of a tall, slim redhead with a too-big mouth and wide eyes looking back at her quizzically. Did my mother look like this when she married…?

'You've never said that before?'

'I'll show you a photo if you like.'

Sara's eyes widened. 'I didn't think there were any!'

'Well, I put them away…it made me feel…' He cleared his throat and looked embarrassed. 'I put them away,' he admitted gruffly. 'I find it hard to talk about your mother, and you are very like her…and not just in looks.'

'That might be the nicest thing you've ever said to me,' she murmured emotionally as the door swung open in response to George's discreet tap.

Sara blinked. The hospital room had been transformed: just about every surface in the room was filled with flowers of every description, and the heavy perfume that hung in the air was simply glorious. As Sara gazed about her in astonishment Charles, dressed in a kilt, of all things, struck up the wedding march on his electric guitar.

Encouraged by the slight pressure of her father's hand on her arm, she moved forward towards the spot where Sean stood. As she looked at him her panic levels reached epic proportions. I might be the only person to spontaneously asphyxiate, she thought as she struggled to draw air into her oxygen-depleted lungs. It was a claim to fame she could do without.

In a beautifully tailored dark grey suit, his tall figure effortlessly dominated the room... Or is it just me he's dominating? a quizzical voice in her head wondered. He looked truly magnificent.

He turned.

Sara was totally paralysed by the expression in his eyes as they slid over her. The smouldering glow encompassed pride, passion and a fierce possessiveness that transfixed her.

As her eyes clung to his slowly her panic receded and a strange calm descended over her. She handed the charming bouquet of old-fashioned cabbage roses and gypsophila her father had hesitantly provided her with as they had left the house to Angeline and took the last step.

Despite all her expectations, once the ceremony began she forgot it wasn't real and made her declarations in a quiet, clear voice that rang with sincerity. Even more amazingly it was in Sean's deep voice the occasional unlikely emotional tremor emerged.

'You may now kiss the bride.'

'You look absolutely lovely,' Sean whispered as he leaned down to take her lips. His kiss received the applause it deserved from the small band of onlookers.

The reception consisted of champagne, Charles's tiny canapés, which melted in your mouth, and strawberries and cream, which were served with panache.

'Well, I must admit,' Hilary remarked to Sara when she had drawn her to one side, 'that I was disappointed that David wasn't able to perform the ceremony, but this vicar was quite splendid, such a resonant voice,' she added admiringly. 'I can almost see him on the stage...such presence.'

Sara, who could also see the vicar on stage but was trying not to, swallowed a strawberry whole.

'Went down the wrong way,' she explained to her concerned stepmother. 'It's fine now.' She dabbed her watering eyes with a tissue.

'And so good-looking.'

Sara's anxiety levels soared. Where was Sean when you needed him…? Talking to the prettiest girl in the room. That would be right, she thought, tearing her eyes away as Angeline threw back her head and laughed hard at something he had said.

'Who is?'

'The vicar, my dear. I wonder where Sean found him?'

Sara didn't know where to look. 'Actually, I think a friend of Dad's recommended him. Doesn't Angeline look gorgeous in that dress?' she added in a desperate attempt to steer the conversation away from the vicar.

'Indeed, lovely girl. I was just telling Charles that he'd better marry her before someone else snaps her up.'

'I can't imagine Charles married.'

'Well, you could have said the same about Sean, my dear. The bigger they are, the harder they fall.'

Sara discovered something she urgently needed to do the other side of the room.

The celebrations were necessarily short. Even so Hilary looked desperately tired, but you were inclined to overlook this because of the air of deep contentment she exuded.

Sara pretended to be unaware that Sean's eyes were shadowing her every move as she wandered around the enormous living room admiring some of the beautiful things.

She stopped saying anything when she could no longer stand the forced and unnatural sound of her own comments. Keeping up a flow of small talk with no help from the person you were talking to was enough to make the most laid-back of people feel a bit strained.

'I never knew lying could be so exhausting!' Her exhausted sigh was completely unfeigned as she sank wearily into the luxurious upholstery of a soft leather sofa; like most of the furniture in the room, it was sleek and modern.

'Do you regret it?' Sean asked bluntly.

Sara didn't have to think about it. 'Goodness, no.' She shook her head. 'Did you see Hilary's face?'

'No, I was looking at yours.'

Her eyelashes came down in a concealing curtain. She had less success concealing the husky tremor in her voice. 'This is an incredible home.'

He looked in a desultory fashion around the room. No expense had been spared. His fixtures and fittings were top of the range, the very latest technology could offer. The minimalist furnishings were equally cutting edge. The paintings on the walls were all by up-and-coming artists whose work was considered to be a good investment.

He felt no personal attachment to any of them. It had never struck him before how soulless the place was.

'It's an investment, not a home.'

'I suppose a lot of people look on property that way,' she said dubiously.

The stern outline of his sensuous lips softened. 'But not you?'

'I've not got any business sense at all,' she admitted apologetically. 'Dad would do far better to leave his money to you. Not that I expect he's going to pop his clogs for some time yet.' Her eyes widened. 'Oh, I didn't...!'

She glanced across at him anxiously—a reference, even a joking one, to death seemed in very bad taste when Hilary's future was hanging in the balance. Sean didn't look offended, but he did look...actually, she couldn't quite figure out what the message was in those stunning grey eyes of his, but it made her shiver and breathe a little faster.

'And that wouldn't bother you...?'

She shrugged. 'Not especially. I sometimes think money is more trouble than it's worth, but I expect I'd feel quite different if there was any real chance of me ever being really poor,' she admitted with a self-derisive grimace. 'It's easy to say money isn't important when you've got an indecent amount of it...or your family has.'

'You're an extraordinary woman, Sara Garvey.'

The sound of the unfamiliar name made her blink. 'Oh,' she laughed uneasily. 'I suppose I'll have to get used to hearing that.' And then get used to *not* hearing it all over again. There was a pensive expression on her face as she slipped the thin stole from her shoulders and looped it over the back of the sofa.

'Lots of married women don't take their husband's name, or choose to link the two these days.'

'Yeah, but all those double barrels can get a bit cumbersome. In the second generation names could become unmanageably long.'

'True.'

'I suppose we are obliged to act as a married couple for a while...?' It struck her forcibly that these were details that anyone with half a brain would have worked out ahead of time. Suddenly worried, she sought his reassurance. 'Only *Dad* knows the truth, nobody else...except us, of course.'

'That's not totally true. Actually, only I know the full truth.'

'How do you mean...?'

'The stripogram vicar's career has taken an upward turn. He's got a small role in a film they're shooting in Canada.'

'That's great, he seemed really nice. When does he leave?'

'No, you don't understand what I'm saying, Sara.' There was nothing new in that—he'd been saying things to her she hadn't heard almost non-stop! Some time very soon he was going to have to do something about that. 'He's already there.'

'He can't be, he was...' She watched Sean shake his head

slowly from side to side. She gulped. 'Then who was that who…?'

'Married us. A brother of a mate of mine from uni.'

She didn't want to believe the incredible explanation that was solidifying in her head. It was entirely too far-fetched and silly, not to mention terrifying!

'I don't suppose he did drama at university, did he?'

Sean shook his head. 'Theology and then he became a…'

'Oh, my God!'

The next thing she had her head between her knees and Sean was kneeling beside her.

'Take some deep breaths. You'll feel better.'

It would take more than deep breaths to make her feel better! 'Let go!' she snapped, shrugging off the hand he had placed on the back of her head.

'Am I dreaming or are you telling me we are actually married? Legally married.'

'Yes. When I explained the circumstances to him yesterday, our vicar obtained a special licence for us, so the marriage is valid.'

'But *how*? *Why*…? I just can't take this in,' she cried, massaging her pounding temples with her thumbs.

'I'll get you some water.'

'Water!' she shrieked. She gazed in incredulous disbelief at his impassive countenance. 'I don't want water…?'

'You're right, brandy would be better.'

Sara lunged forward and caught his arm. 'I do not want brandy!' she gritted. 'I suppose I should be grateful you saw fit to tell me now, not in a few months' time! I want to hear an explanation, *now*.'

'Even if George hadn't come up with the vicar scam you'd have been willing to get married to make Mum happy, wouldn't you…?'

An image of Hilary's serene, contented smile drifted before Sara's eyes.

'Maybe I would,' she conceded. 'But I would have been making an informed decision. My *choice*, don't you get it? You bypassed that, you made the decision for me, you manipulated me and that is totally unforgivable. You knew. I think even if you were working on a strict need-to-know basis I actually did *need to know*!'

'I did what I thought was the best and when you calm down a little you'll see that,' he contended calmly.

He was mad, that was the only explanation—he was stark, staring bonkers. 'I'm not going to calm down!' she shrieked, incandescent with rage.

'If you think about it rationally.' One look at her combative posture made it obvious this was highly unlikely. 'Nothing has changed essentially. Like you just said, we would have been obliged to give the impression of living together as husband and wife.'

'And now we *are* husband and wife.' The full impact of that reality hit her and she swayed. 'I thought you wanted to get married once!' she accused shrilly.

'That is my intention,' he revealed sardonically.

'Then you want this to be permanent?' She gasped. Her heart was racing so fast she could hardly breathe. He wasn't saying…no, he *couldn't* be…

'It's possible we're just anticipating something that would have happened anyway?' he suggested.

'What do you mean?'

'Well, you weren't strictly honest with me when you said it wasn't likely you could get pregnant, were you?'

Sara felt the colour rise up her neck until her entire face was burning. 'There was no need for you to know. If anything had happened, I would have coped with it.'

And she still would if anything did, she thought grimly. She didn't need a husband who had married her just because of a baby. She wanted a husband who was madly in love with her and to think for one second there she'd foolishly allowed herself to believe...!

Sean listened to her militant declaration in silence.

'I see...so it's all right for you to make a decision on my behalf...?' His jaw tightened. 'Why do the words double and standard spring to mind?'

Sara gritted her teeth in sheer frustration. 'It's not the same thing at all.'

'Why aren't I surprised to hear you say that?' he drawled.

'Besides, nobody gets pregnant the first time.' As soon as the words were out of her mouth Sara knew she'd lost all credibility as a rational human being.

'I've got a god-daughter, she's ten next week. I'm sure she'd be willing to explain the rudimentary points of the fertility cycle.'

'Very funny.' Sean has a god-daughter—*why didn't I know that...*? But then why would I? I've barely even touched his life. In the middle of this gloomy acknowledgement it quite suddenly came to her, the thing that had been niggling her, the missing detail.

'How could you know...?' One of the few things she hadn't given him access to was her diary. In every other way she'd stripped herself bare, emotionally and literally!

'When I went to pick up your stuff that *Rupert* had packed.' For some reason she couldn't begin to fathom at the moment he pronounced the name with real loathing. As far as she knew he wasn't homophobic; in fact he had a tolerant live-and-let-live attitude that she'd always approved of.

'I had a little look around while he was busy rifling through your knicker drawer.' Again she heard the distaste in his voice, more controlled but still there. 'The calendar on your kitchen wall with the days circled in red...?' He watched her eyes widen. 'It didn't take a lot of figuring out.'

'Good God, what did you do, walk around with a hidden camera?'

'I didn't need to.' He tapped the side of his head with his finger. 'Have you forgotten I have a photographic memory?'

'I thought Hilary was exaggerating.'

'She wasn't, my remarkable brain is crammed full of totally useless information. Anyone needs the South Eastern line train timetable for nineteen eighty-nine and it's all here...' He tapped his head once more. 'So, *are you*?'

The abrupt change of subject threw her. 'Am I what?'

An exasperated sigh hissed through his clenched teeth. *'Are you pregnant?'* he elucidated loudly.

'Shouldn't you have asked that before you took such a drastic action?'

'Did I say I did it because of that?'

'You didn't have to...you've nothing to gain financially from this, and as the only other reason people get married is *love*, which clearly doesn't apply here, that only leaves...' She shrugged. This had to be about a baby.

'Why can't I be in love with you?'

Was he trying to be cruel? 'Very funny!' she drawled.

His nostrils flared and a faint white line appeared around his sensual lips. 'You think the idea of me loving you is a joke?'

'A very bad one.'

It took him several seconds before he trusted himself to speak. 'And I suppose it'll be hilarious if you're pregnant too?'

Sara blushed. 'I've told you, it's too early to say,' she mumbled. 'But even if I am,' she added, gaining confidence, 'it's nothing whatever to do with you.'

'Even *you* must recognise that that was an incredibly stupid thing to say. If you are pregnant it is my responsibility,' he said heavily.

Joy, delight, she would have welcomed those responses,

but not *responsibility*. Her baby, if there ever was one, deserved more than that, and so did she!

'I was there too...'

'I remember.'

The brooding expression in his silver-flecked eyes produced the increasingly familiar heavy, dragging sensation low in her belly. Sara fought stubbornly against the silken bonds of sexual thrall.

'Don't women just know when they're pregnant? Aren't there signs? *Nausea*...' His eyes dropped to the rounded contours of her breasts. *'Tenderness...?'*

Sara recalled the nausea she had experienced that morning and the increased sensitivity of her nipples, but that could have a lot to do with the fact she'd been walking around in an almost constant state of sexual arousal for the past few days.

'My God, anyone would think you'd been reading a book,' she sneered. For one brief, unguarded moment Sean looked embarrassed. Her jaw dropped. 'My, God, you have, haven't you...?'

'Actually I looked the subject up on the internet. It was quite informative. If you are pregnant you'll need someone to look after you.'

'And you're volunteering...? What will Penny think about that, or have you traded her in for a newer model?'

'Before your jealousy leads you to say something you'll really regret, let me put you straight on a few things.'

'Jealousy!' She tossed her head scornfully and the flower that had been clipped above her ear became detached.

Sean, with a dazzling display of speed and co-ordination, caught it before it hit the floor. He raised it to his face and inhaled before threading it into the buttonhole of his jacket.

'You're sick with it,' he declared confidently. 'And a deeply destructive emotion it is, too.'

Sara longed to slap the smug, know-it-all look off his face. 'I'm sick, all right…sick of you!' she wailed.

'Firstly Penny is not my mistress, she is my indispensable right hand at work.'

'I didn't see any *Penny* when I was working at your place,' she snarled.

Sean's sensual lips compressed in a disapproving line. 'What, the entire half a day, you mean…? In that case, clearly she doesn't work there.'

Sara flushed.

'While Mum has been ill Penny has been running her butt off to cover for me. We produced our first full-length feature this year.'

'I thought you only did TV.'

'I'm flattered you noticed. Actually this is a new departure for us. It was not exactly a low-risk venture—for every mass-appeal, low-budget British movie that makes good there are dozens that sink without trace.'

'Did you sink?' She didn't for one second think he had; Sean exuded a quality that couldn't be bought or acquired. You looked at him and couldn't possibly imagine him failing at anything he set his mind to.

'Actually when the film premièred in Cannes it aroused a lot of interest.' Modesty forbade him to mention the more concrete prizes it had garnered also, like the prestigious award. 'I had some meetings scheduled there last week with distributors, Penny stepped in for me.' The admiration in his voice was unmistakable, as was his enthusiasm for his subject. 'The upshot is she pulled off a fantastic distribution deal!'

'So she works for you and she's good at what she does…' *Damn her.* 'It has been known for the boss to sleep with his protégé!'

'Penny is married.'

Which made him a lying swine who slept with married

women. 'A married woman who tells you what colour knickers she's wearing over the phone. *Nice.*'

'Now I know she didn't do that!'

'She *would* have,' Sara delivered mutinously.

'The only clothing she could possibly have mentioned was her shirt—when she interviewed for the job she was easily the least qualified person there. She claims that the only reason I gave it to her was because she stuck in my mind because she arrived wearing her shirt inside out.'

More like it was what was inside the shirt that influenced his decision, Sara decided cynically.

'So it's become a superstition thing. When we need to be lucky she turns her top inside out for luck.'

God, it all fitted! 'I suppose I might have misunderstood,' she mumbled.

'So when she rings you'll be nice...?'

'I'm always nice and I won't be here.'

'Sara, we're married—that's not going to change.'

'I know a lawyer who might dispute that.'

'You don't know a lawyer,' he contradicted confidently. 'And we both know you're not going to divorce me.'

Sara found his smile, presumably meant to be reasonable, unaccountably chilling.

'You're stuck with me for the duration. Like the man said, we can do this the easy way or the hard way, and, let's face it, it's going to be *really* hard for you to keep your hands off me.'

His arrogant pronouncement took her breath away. The awful part was that he was right!

'I'm out of here!' she sobbed suddenly.

Sean grabbed her arm and spun her back. The impetus catapulted her straight into him. Her breasts were crushed against the firm barrier of his chest. After a moment's shock she felt her body relax into him; it was not something she had any control over.

It was like, she mused weakly, when you held your breath. You could do it just so long, you might even do it so well you passed out, but once those autonomic responses took over you were greedily gulping in the oxygen—Sean being her oxygen of this analogy.

He had certainly become as essential to her as the air she breathed.

'I know this because it wouldn't just be hard for me, it would be *hell*!' he pronounced forcefully.

The raw rasp in his deep, throaty voice was enough to send Sara's body temperature up several degrees. She kept her head down, refusing to acknowledge the heat and the prickles of sexual longing crawling over her skin.

'This is you making the best of things again?'

'This is me being honest.'

When she wouldn't look at him he took her chin and wrenched her face around to him.

'Don't you think it's about time you were the same, Sara? This marriage may not have come about in a strictly conventional way, but, given a bit of give and take...'

'Me giving—you taking.' She jerked away from the long brown fingers circling her chin.

'I see no reason it shouldn't work.' None that he was about to acknowledge, anyhow. 'And if you're thinking about *Rupert*, forget it. He's smooth, I'll give him that,' he reflected grimly, 'but he's not your type.'

Sara found the introduction of her neighbour into the conversation at this crucial moment confusing. She was even more confused about the depth of loathing in Sean's voice when he said the other man's name.

'My type being...?'

'*Me!*' he declared with breathtaking insolence.

'Well, I'd take issue with that.' She tried and failed to sound entertained and not disastrously turned on by his arrogant claim. 'But actually you're right, I'm not Rupert's type.' This time her amusement was genuine.

'*Sure* you're not.' Sean couldn't imagine her not being any man's type.

Sara shot him a sly look from under her lashes. 'But *you* are,' she told him softly.

'You say that now, but...' Sean froze. His mouth opened once, then again, but nothing emerged. 'Are you saying he's...' he gulped '...not straight?'

Sara slowly shook her head. 'You were jealous,' she murmured wonderingly. 'It's quite a coincidence but someone told me, quite recently as it happens, that jealousy is a destructive emotion.'

Flags of colour banded his high slashing cheeks as his eyes slid from hers. He lifted a hand and dragged it across his eyes. 'Is it so surprising I'm jealous?' he demanded aggressively.

'Quite frankly, Sean, it's bloody amazing!' Didn't jealousy imply a certain degree of caring...?

'Well, what do you expect, woman? The way you were laughing with him on the phone—you don't laugh like that with me!' His resentful eyes flickered hungrily over her astonished face.

'There are quite a few things I do with you that I don't do with Rupert. I thought men could tell about things like that...I mean, he's not screamingly camp or anything, but I noticed right off.'

'Yes...well...' Sean cleared his throat and looked self-conscious. 'Maybe I did jump to conclusions,' he growled. 'You can't tell me you haven't figured out I'm absolutely out of my mind crazy about you,' he grated abruptly.

Sara drew a startled breath. The shocks were coming so thick and fast she felt kind of floaty. She held up her hand. With a weird objectivity she noticed it trembling violently.

'Do you mind going back a bit there?' she requested hoarsely.

'How far back?'

'Around about the part where you say you are *crazy* about me will do. Are you *really*?' she whispered wonderingly. Her expression hardened. 'Or are you talking about sex?'

'Incredible, isn't it?' A fierce grin briefly split his tense features. 'But I'm talking the whole caring, sharing, forsaking-all-others package here. I know you think me loving you is some sort of joke... Maybe I deserve that, but, God, I do love you, Sara, and if you're pregnant I'll love our baby. I think you could love me too...' he swallowed '...if you could bring yourself to trust me.'

Something detonated softly inside her skull; the implosion created a numbness. Numb she could cope with, Sara decided, covering her face with her hands. The rest...! It felt as if nothing short of ten years of therapy would sort out that!

'This isn't happening to me.'

Clearly she'd stopped being able to differentiate between reality and fantasy. I've wanted Sean for so long it's affected my brain, she decided.

'*Hell!* I knew I shouldn't have said anything...forget I did, we're doing fine as we are.'

Sara had never heard anything remotely resembling panic in Sean's voice, and she'd never expected to. This glimpse of his vulnerability moved her deeply. Her fingers slid down, revealing her wide turquoise eyes but still concealing the lower part of her face.

'You know that's not true, Sean, this isn't fine.' Her hands fell away. 'I have to know,' she quivered. 'Are you saying these things because you think I might be pregnant?'

'I'm saying these things because they're true and I'm an idiot,' he declared bitterly. 'I was so busy trying to preserve my *bachelor freedom* it was a long time before I could even admit to myself how I felt about you. I told myself you were way trouble, and you are,' he reflected with a loving look that made her knees shake. 'But it's the sort of trouble I need. I don't want a low-maintenance mistress, I want you, Sara. All the things about you that drove me mad are the things I love about you. Every time I tried to tell you how I felt, George would pop up like some overweight, evil bad fairy.'

'*You love me...!*' Perhaps if she said it often enough it would seem real. She was dimly conscious that she wasn't responding to this declaration the way she did in her dreams, but then Sean wasn't either.

Did love normally make people look as though they were in acute pain? she wondered, looking at his taut, strained face.

'Why do you keep saying it like it's some big surprise?' he growled. 'Why do you think I arranged for us to be ma...'

Sara scanned his impossibly handsome face; he looked like a kid who'd been caught with his hand in the cookie jar.

'You *arranged* for us to be married...? I thought you didn't have any choice? Dad's fake vicar's in Canada.'

'You really do constantly underestimate your dad's resourcefulness. Do you really think *George Stean* couldn't produce a fake vicar if he needed to? The man has more resources than many small countries I could mention,' he declared cynically. 'We are talking one little vicar here, not change in our monetary policy, which he can do with a well-timed editorial.'

'I get the point,' Sara breathed. 'God, you make him sound quite...*sinister*,' she gasped, realising with a sense of shock the breadth and scope of her father's influence on business affairs. It also brought home how much Sean had turned down when he hadn't accepted George's bribe.

'Let's just say it's a whole lot easier to have him on your side than not.'

'And is he on your side, Sean?'

'Quite frankly, angel, I could care less. When I said I had the vicar thing covered he didn't ask any questions, which was all I wanted. I didn't intend telling you until later. *Later*,' he added with a snort of derision, 'being some indefinite point when you'd realised you couldn't live without me. When it came down to it, you looked at me so trustingly, I couldn't keep my mouth shut.' His head fell back, exposing the convulsive movement of the muscles in his throat.

'God, I knew deep down it was a crazy thing to do, only I was scared witless of losing you and I kept thinking of Rupert hovering in the wings... I felt nearly as bad as when George first told me you were pregnant.'

'You felt bad about that?'

Sean pressed his fists together until she heard his knuckles crunch. 'Pretty bad, as in sick to my stomach. I wanted to kill the creep who had put you in that position, which is pretty ironic considering I neglected to protect you too.' He gave a bitter laugh. 'This wasn't the best way to show you I'm not like George, was it? *God!* I've really blown it, haven't I?'

The anguish on his face made Sara's heart feel as though it were breaking. 'I don't think you're like him; in fact, I *know* you're not, but you have to promise me one thing right here.'

'Anything!' Sean said, meaning it.

'You'll never exclude me from any decisions concerning our future together ever again.'

'We *have* a future together...?'

'I suppose I could live without you, but...' Her voice cracked emotionally. 'I don't want to!'

'What are you trying to say?' His mind had still not got out of first gear.

'I'm not trying, I'm saying I love you, Sean. I can't imagine ever *not* loving you, idiot!'

With a groan he gathered her in his arms. 'I just kept clinging to the hope…' He rained hot kisses over her face and neck. 'Sara. *My Sara.*' He smiled, liking the sound of it. 'I love you so much!'

'How much?' she whispered, sinking her fingers into his dark hair.

'Perhaps I could show you,' he growled, looking more like the Sean she knew.

Sara smiled. 'I'm relying on it.' She laughed delightedly as he swept her up into his arms.

George Stean waited impatiently for the lift to respond to his summons. He had the paperwork in his briefcase that would hand control of Stean Holdings to his stepson.

He wasn't taking no for an answer this time and if Sean got stubborn he had taken out insurance. He had persuaded a doctor friend to forge a fake medical report that said he would be putting his life at risk if he didn't make some serious lifestyle changes.

Smiling to himself, he moved forward as the doors slid silently open. He stopped in his tracks. The lift was already occupied and the occupants, locked in a passionate embrace, didn't seem inclined to vacate any time soon.

'I thought you had a phobia of enclosed spaces…?'

The sound of her father's voice made Sara shriek. Flushed with embarrassment, she broke free of her husband's arms; a quick glance in his direction told her he wasn't suffering a similar awkwardness.

'Dad, what are you doing here?'

'Besides ruining a beautiful moment,' Sean drawled.

Sara shot him a warning look but he grinned imperturbably back.

'I had some business with Sean.'

'Not now, George, we were on our way to the hospital.'

'Couldn't be better, I'm heading that way myself. We can talk on the way. Now, I know we've had our differences, but despite that I'm still eager to have you take over from me...no strings, of course. In fact, I'm glad you're not really married...far too much divorce these days...'

'But we are.'

George stared open-mouthed from one to the other; a slow smile spread over his face. 'The hell you are!' He grinned. 'You mean the vicar chap was kosher? Ah-h-h, that explains him getting a bit weird when I...never mind about that. Well, son of a gun...congratulations!' He beamed, pumping Sean's hand up and down.

'We'll see you at the hospital, George...'

George wondered at the younger man's coldness. 'You didn't actually think I meant that stuff about getting custody of Sara's baby, did you? You know it was a joke.'

'You threatened to do that?' Sara breathed wrathfully.

'He didn't tell you?' Sara could see her father was clearly regretting he had opened this particular can of worms.

'I can see you two want to be alone,' he said, tapping the side of his nose. 'I'll leave you both to it. If you have a minute or two, though, Sean, you might like to have a little look through these.' He dropped the document case into Sean's hand.

'What the hell's in this?'

'Your future, my boy.'

'Oh, God, he's trying to give me the company again!' Sean groaned.

'It would be an opportunity for you to stamp your own identity on it. I'm sure you don't agree with some of the things Dad's been doing.'

'Are you kidding? He's—' He stopped. 'Are you doing a number on me?'

'Would I do that?'

'You're a Stean, my love.'

'Regretting it…?' she asked, grabbing a handful of shirt and yanking him towards her.

'Hardly!' Sean breathed with flattering fervour.

'Why didn't you tell me about Dad's threats?'

'I wouldn't have let him hurt you. Besides…' His eyes lovingly scanned her face. 'I got sidetracked. It was those pink knickers of yours.'

Sara blushed. 'Actually, for once Dad's right. I haven't been in a lift without getting out a gibbering wreck for a long time…in fact *ever*! Why do you suppose…?'

'Maybe you know you don't have anything to worry about whilst I'm around. I won't let anything hurt you, my love, not ever.'

Maybe that was it. She felt safe and protected…he lifted her eyes to his…oh, and loved, *definitely* loved. He'd proved that to her in many, *many* ways the previous night.

'You could be right.'

'Let's test the theory,' Sean murmured, reaching for the button. As the door closed he gathered her in his arms. 'One for the road, my darling…?'

Sara sighed. 'Oh, yes, please!'

EPILOGUE

ALL eyes in the church were on the small group progressing with state-like calm up the aisle to the rousing strains of the wedding march. Numerous sighs followed and admiring gasps followed their progress.

Sara was oblivious to it all, the people, the music, everything but the broad shoulders of the tall, distinguished figure waiting for them.

They had almost reached him when he turned. His spectacular eyes widened fractionally as he saw her. A silent message passed between them in the way it did when two people had developed an almost telepathic rapport.

Sean felt his chest swell with pride. *His Sara*—he couldn't believe he was this lucky!

Sara felt a rush of joy so intense it hurt. The unconditional love shining in Sean's eyes brought tears to hers. She couldn't believe she was this lucky.

The bride turned and handed Sara the bouquet. Sara smiled encouragingly before stepping back to a spot where she could watch the ceremony and keep an eye on the small page who had managed to get himself wedged underneath a pew during the rehearsal.

Sara smiled when Angeline began to speak. Her friend had been convinced her nervousness would reveal itself in some embarrassingly inappropriate manner, like hiccups or floods of manic laughter. Nothing could have been farther from the truth. Her responses had an emotional clarity that brought tears to many an eye of those gathered to celebrate the union.

The groom's responses, though equally resonant, lacked

his usual buoyant confidence, but they were delivered with a gravity that was even more attractive. Listening to him affirm his love, Sara couldn't help her gaze straying to Sean. She discovered he was watching her; he smiled and she felt dizzy with love.

There was quite a lot of laughter later when the youthful page looked up at Sara and observed, 'Your eyes are leaking!' in a loud, penetrating treble.

'So they are.' She sniffed, relieved when the kid's harassed-looking parent appeared to take charge.

'I don't know how you managed to keep him still, but whatever it was you did I'm grateful,' she breathed.

'Bribery…?'

'That sometimes works,' his mother agreed calmly. 'If I can keep him from destroying anything or falling into something for another half-hour the photos will be done and we're home free,' she said, displaying her crossed fingers to Sara. 'I've got everything else crossed too.'

Sara laughed as she gave a moan and set off after her hyperactive son, who was climbing on an ancient headstone.

She gave a watery smile when Sean appeared at her side with a tissue.

'This is getting ridiculous. I can't go more than an hour without bursting into tears.'

'Everyone cries at weddings,' he soothed, drawing her a little away from the happy crush of people who had spilled higgledy-piggledy out of the church.

'Weddings, yes, but cartoons on TV, songs…?'

'That was scary,' he admitted, recalling the occasion he had arrived home to find his pregnant wife curled up on the sofa in floods of tears. All sorts of horrors had run through his head before she had revealed it had been the actions of a purple character on a children's television show that had reduced her to an emotional basket case.

'Never mind,' he soothed, placing a loving hand over his wife's ever-expanding abdomen. 'Not long now.'

'Do I look ridiculous in this get-up?' she asked, peering down at her bulky body clothed in cerise pink satin—Angeline's choice.

She had got used to looking like a whale, but a pink whale—that upset her.

'You look beautiful,' he announced with fierce conviction. 'And you're mine…' he added with husky wonder.

'God, I'm going to start crying again,' Sara sniffed.

Believing the theory that said a person couldn't cry when being kissed, Sean pressed a long, lingering kiss to his wife's lovely lips.

The sultry look in her eyes when he lifted his head took his breath away.

'Have I told you recently how much I love you?' he asked.

'Yes, but I have no objection to hearing it again,' Sara admitted huskily.

'There you are, darlings!'

'*Later,*' Sean whispered to Sara before turning with a smile to his mother, who was jogging across the grass, her hand pressed on the crown of her big hat to prevent it blowing away.

Sara didn't think she'd ever be able to see Hilary like this—happy and bubbling over with healthy vitality—and not marvel at the miracle medical science and the generosity of a person the other side of the world had brought about.

'Mum, be careful—the grass is wet, you'll slip,' Sean warned as she drew level with them.

'Don't be such a fusspot, Sean,' his parent responded crossly. 'I've had enough of being wrapped in cotton wool to last me several lifetimes.'

'Point taken, Mum.'

'What, no argument?' Hilary exclaimed. 'My, Sara, I think you've tamed the man.'

Sara lifted her eyes to the tall figure of the man beside her; her heart swelled. 'I don't want to tame him. I like him just the way he is.'

She didn't see Hilary reach in her handbag for a tissue to dab the emotional tear from her cheek. Or hear the older woman say, 'I'll tell the photographer you're just coming,' before slipping quietly away.

All she was conscious of was the bright flame in the eyes of the man she loved to distraction. She remained in this spellbound condition until the child in her belly landed a particularly sharp kick.

'Ouch!' She winced.

Sean immediately bent over her, concern on his face. 'Are you all right?'

'Fine,' Sara promised quickly. 'He's just woken up. Feel.' She took his hand and placed it on her belly.

His eyes widened as their child obligingly kicked again—no matter how often he felt it, he never failed to be moved by the sheer wonder of it.

'He's getting strong.'

'Like his father.'

'And impatient.'

'Again like his father.'

'Then we'll be a real family.' A grin spread over his face. 'Will you listen to me? Hell, Mum's right, I'm domesticated. What do you know? Pipe and slippers, here I come,' he joked, displaying no regret as he contemplated the demise of his bachelor freedom.

Sara gave a contented smile. She knew deep down that, no matter how many children they had, she was never going to lose her untamed lover.

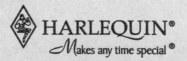

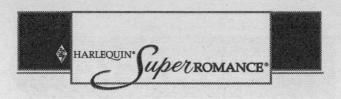